Chocolate's

Seventh Day

Soliloquy Vol. 1

<u>Special Edition</u>

S. S. SUGGS

NOTES BY VIRGIE, INC.

ISBN: 978-1-7369682-0-8

Cover design by: Art Painter
Printed in the United States of America

TABLE OF CONTENT

Dedication

This book is dedicated to my mother. I thank my mother, Virgie, for being herself and never viewing herself as people saw her. She was bold, loud, loving, funny, witty, and a friend to many. She never gave up on anyone. She always saw the blessing in the ability to share what little she had. Now that's real love

When I think about who was the most dedicated in my life. I must recognize the mother of mothers, my grandmother Marion. She was selfless and committed to loving everyone. She showed compassion to the friendless, the homeless, the helpless and the less fortunate. She will forever whole the title of SHEro of my life. If I could give an ounce of what she gave to so many, then that would be what I call, REAL LOVE!

Love Shared…

I want to thank my family.

To my own Mr. Christopher, thank you for always allowing me to seek my own way, for putting up with all of my "great ideas and for your support and encouragement. You held me together so many times, when I fell apart. For that, I am eternally grateful.

To my daughter, thank you for encouraging me to write and write and write. You never give up on me even when I give up on myself. You always push me beyond my limits. You are the reason I can say proudly, "I am a mother!" You are the greatest gift next to life I could provide, nurture, and love unconditionally.

To my Dad, thanks for all you do. You are my hero and thanks for always coming to the rescue.

To Lisha, you already know how I feel. You carry me through whatever journey I take. You are my big sister, my best friend, and the only person I admire. I love you CuzSis, so get ready to receive all you have given.

To Shakeela, Baseemah, and Tinika, thank you all for allowing me to advise, counsel, and love you. Even when I was not perfect, you never judged me. When they see me, they will always see you!

I want to thank those special to my journey of growth.

To Monica, I would not be what I am today if you did not sacrifice for my dream to be fulfilled. You give without any expectation of receiving. You are my soundboard, prayer warrior, speaker of truth, my Louise, and more.

To Anthony, thank you my best friend. I would give my feet to so that you may walk in style. But, knowing you like I do; you would never take them.

To Zerina, thank you for trusting me with your "word" and now the world knows. We are off to the races.

To my brothers, cousins, and friends, please know there are "no limits" to what we can do.

Introduction

"I don't want to wake up from here. To wake up means this right here has ended. How do I wake up from the touch of Mr. Noble's embrace?

Wake up from the feeling of our bodies connecting, this passion we share. To wake up, I would be reminded of the smell and the soft touch of his skin next to mine. Wake up from the grasp of Noble's hands squeezing my thighs, playing with this cymbal in my muscle, the pinch of my cushion, and the pull of my pillows. Why wake up to the reality of our time ending? Or the mere fact that this moment will leave my memory?

I want to stay here, right now, in this space, with him. I don't want to wake up, I don't want to sleep. I want him to hit my bell softly, slow, then fast and quick. Allow no sleep to occur just motion and motions of pain, then pleasure. Waking up will not be an option if we focus on the things in demand. In and out and out and in, the uncontrollable shiver of legs, the ache in my back, and the need to breathe or scream with my release.

The relationship between Virgie and Noble heats up. They discover what they need to keep their relationship full of passion and love. This discovery is not without the twists, turns, highs, and lows that are involved in relationships. Noble is a strong black man who appears to have it all together. Virgie is an independent black woman who knows what she likes and needs in her life. Nevertheless, there is still something mysterious about these lovebirds.

This book will journey through the things that make people silent. It will allow us to lose ourselves in the sensual encounters of intimacy and to spark the flame of a loving conversation between a man and his woman.

Foreword

You're about to enter the story of Virgie. She is all of us. A woman of the 21st century trying to balance family, friends, a successful career, and new love. Noble, the love of her life, is a mysterious man. He is strong, successful, and sensual beyond belief. His wish is to fulfill her every desire but is that enough? Along with Virgie and Noble, the author introduces an entire cast of characters that will keep you laughing and crying throughout the story.

From their hilarious interactions with one another to the heart break of life, each person represents a family member or friend that we can all relate to. The author takes us through the highs and lows of new relationships. The difficulties of finding the balance of who we are as individuals and who we are as couples.

Virgie and Noble's love story is one filled with sensual twists and turns. It is filled with erotic fantasies and sexual experiments shared through powerful imagery. It is a story of strong Black love, a strong Black family, and a Strong black woman. Their love is patient and kind. But most of all it is sensual and delights in the pleasure of its partner. Their love is difficult but most of all it is beautiful as it blossoms throughout the week.

I hope you enjoy the story of Virgie. May she give you the courage to create your own soliloquy.

JLS

About the Author

S. S. Suggs knows firsthand what sensual encounters can do for romantic relationships. The author is well sought after for relationship advice and ideas for exchanges of intimacy. S. S. Suggs is a graduate with a bachelor's degree in Sociology (the study of human behavior) and a master's degree in Arts and Science.

S. S. Suggs is a storyteller who enjoys exploring the imagery of sensual encounters, bringing sensual encounters to life through her words. It is with a background in human behavior and arts and sciences, the author uses her education to help people through the complexity of relationships daily. With a love for details and descriptive language, the author takes an approach on word play to audiences from all backgrounds.

SATURDAY

"Good morning, good morning is what I say to myself every morning."

I slept so well last night. I didn't toss or turn not one single time. I should probably send Mr. Noble a quick note to thank him for that, nope I am not going to do it. Noble already thinks he is the bomb dot com. You know what, I might do it anyway. He likes it when I pump up his head with compliments of how great he is. He stays full of himself. Noble acts like he doesn't like all of the fanfare, but I know he does. He lights up. His cheeks turn rosy red. He is my big ole chocolate-covered candy drop. This man…. this man has me all sweet on him. Chocolate-covered candy, sweet on him. Noble has my full attention. It's not like he didn't have it before because he did. It's just that this time I'm moving around quite differently after all of these shared moments with him.

I'm still tripping on what happened last night: the rain, the water. It was as if he tapped into my brain and mixed up the right chemistry of emotions. Oooo, I'm smiling too hard. I wonder if anyone saw us or better yet did anyone hear the noise we were making? I need to make a note to myself to check some temperatures when I see my neighbors.

I'm hungry, but I don't feel like cooking. I should call my BFF Natasha Janine so we can go to breakfast together and I can tell her all about last night's adventure. She is always eager and excited to hear the details of me and Mr. Noble's shared moments together. I should call her now before I change my mind.

I bet when I call her, she will answer on the first ring. I knew it.

"Hey girl! Do you want to go to breakfast? Girl, guess what? I was with Noble last night having a shared moment, so I know you want to hear all about it. To be honest, I'm too thirsty! I need to share everything we did in detail last night with you. Yep, I know, you're living through our relationship vicariously, and loving every minute of it. Meet me at Kelle's at 9:30. Okay, girl,

I will see you soon!" Kelle's is a restaurant on the west side of Chicago in the heart of the hood. I love the food there, and their clientele is a wide mix of people.

"Natasha Janine, you will definitely be able to recognize me because I will be the lady smiling from cheek to cheek covering my whole face showing all my teeth. Bye girl don't be mad just be glad you are about to hear all about it."

Today is a day that I will bring out the infamous red pants. I retired those pants, but after last night they will need to make their big comeback. I feel so strong and powerful in them, not to mention that my butt looks round and plump too. I'm going to pair them with my black tank top and add my purple summer scarf for a little something extra. I have to put on my bangles. I need to hear myself and see my wrist jiggling all day to let the people know "I'm out here and here I come." Where are my silver hoops? I think I laid them on the kitchen counter when I came in last night. Nope! There they are, right in my purse. I took them off on my way home from work. These hoop earrings kept getting caught on my scarf yesterday. I have to tell myself, "Virgie, girl get it together because you are around here slow poking." I should wear a nude lipstick, but you know what? Since I'm feeling some kind of way, I will wear bright red lipstick instead. I better get going because before I know it, I will make myself late. Then, I would get on the road breaking all the speed limits. Because I'm driving like a maniac trying to make up the time I wasted.

When I arrive at Kelle's, the parking lot is full like always. Even though Kelle's is a small restaurant it is always filled to capacity. The restaurant is a third-generation family-owned and operated establishment. Kelle's great grandfather who was the first-named Kelle was a creole chef. Kelle told me that the pancake recipe is held in the strictest of confidence and that they have had only three chefs who can make the pancakes outside of his family. All of the chefs have to sign an NDA (non-disclosure agreement). There was one chef who was actually sued which is how Kelle and I came to know each other and then started dating.

I have to park around the corner and walk back to the restaurant. Thank goodness I have on my chucks; they are truly made for walking. The days of wearing heels and walking around in them are over for me, well not really. My feet will not let me walk around in heels anymore. I'm going to keep my heels stored away for the days when I am being dropped off at the door then picked up later. My good friend Maud said to me, "If that man can't drop you at the door and pick you up then he is not worthy of a date in your heels." I always think about that when I go out on a date too. This is the whole reason why I keep flats in my purse. Just in case my date is not the guy Maud described because if I need to change into my flats the date is definitely over.

I walk inside the restaurant and the first person I see is Kelle. Kelle is the owner of this establishment. We used to date a while back but remained friends after an amicable split. I eat here often and because we are friends, I can bypass the line of people waiting. The truth is he still wants me, but I'm dating Noble now so he can just continue lusting after me. When Kelle and I were dating, I always wore these pants when I wanted to get his attention which always worked in my favor.

He loves these red pants.

As I walk up to the hostess booth I say, "Hello Mr. Kelle." He is standing there speaking with a customer. He likes it when I call him mister. For some reason, all the men in my life like it when I call them mister. I don't know why they love to hear it. Nevertheless, I'm all about lifting my men up when this world is committed to tearing them down. Mister for Kelle unequivocally makes him feel empowered.

Kelle stops talking to the customer and says, "Hello, Ms. Virgie! You are looking great, and I see my favorite red pants are out of retirement. May I say welcome back to my favorite pants? Or should I just point out that time has really waited for you because you are aging gracefully?"

"Mr. Kelle, you just saw me last week and said the same thing."

"Ms. Virgie, and if I see you tomorrow, I will say it again. I would love to talk to you when you have time. Nothing fresh just talk."

"Kelle, the way you talk is always an example of more. Have you seen Natasha Janine? She is meeting me here."

"Ms. Virgie, she has been waiting only a couple of minutes. Your friend is in the other room sitting next to the window," as he points in the direction where Natasha Janine is seated.

"Thank you for your help, Mr. Kelle!" I began walking to the other room on the other side of the restaurant to meet with Natasha Janine. I purposely had to walk away switching from left to right letting him see all of this in my infamous red pants. I am determined to show him what he is missing. Too bad so sad but I had to leave the relationship he and I had.

No woman, well not this woman wants to be sitting in a restaurant every day watching you make pancakes. Oh well, enough about Kelle I got to tell Natasha Janine about my Noble. "Hey girl, have you been waiting a long time?" I know she is about to make it as if she had been waiting for hours.

Before she could say it, I say, "You just got here too, you know Kelle already informed me. Natasha Janine you cute, you didn't have to dress up for me."

She is out here looking too cute in a floral dress and some cute red sandals. Natasha Janine is an almond skin color. She is petite and very health conscious. I refer to her as itty bitty. My BFF has on her hoop earrings with her hair in a sloppy ponytail and her nude lipstick. She even has her brows "slayed." Natasha Janine has been my best friend forever and ever. We met in undergrad and both went on to law school together.

"Virgie, I want some blueberry pancakes. Even though I dressed up, I need to know in advance what should be my choice of the beverage I am drinking. Is this information worthy of some hot tea or should I get some milk?"

"Natasha Janine, have I ever given you creamy white milk information?"

"Virg, yes you have! Do remember the time when you told me about that incident at work with the receptionist, or that time you told me about that road trip with those trifling girls, or the time when you told me about you and Kelle's dinner at his aunt house and don't forget about that time when you…"

13

"Girl say it isn't so. Natasha Janine, this information is worthy of some hot brewed tea in a 12-ounce mug."

"Girl let's order some food first I'm starving, and I haven't eaten since yesterday," I say.

This very pretty thin young lady walks towards us. She is tall with long braids in her hair. She stops at our table. I have never seen her here.

She must be a new employee. She says, "Welcome to Kelle's. My name is Mari, and I will be your waitress. Would you like some water, or are you all, ready to order?"

I am the first to greet the young lady by saying, "Hey Mari, we would like to place our order. I will have a short stack of banana pancakes, turkey bacon, well-done turkey sausage links, hash browns, a glass of cranberry juice, no ice, and a cup of Earl Grey hot tea."

Natasha Janine says to me, "Damn big Virg, I swear you are ordering this meal like you are eating for two people."

I responded, "You mad?"

"Girl, hell no I'm eager to know the details, I can't wait to hear this."

I look over at the young lady and say, "Can you tell Sid that this order is for Virgie?" Sid is the chef at the restaurant who I helped to get this job. He is an older black man who has the most beautiful salt and pepper colored beard. He has an athletic build and is as sweet as pie.

I tell her, "Mr. Sid knows exactly how I like my pancakes because we have history."

Mari replies, "I will definitely let him know."

Mari turns to Natasha Janine and says, "What would you like?"

"I would like a tall stack of blueberry pancakes and an order of pork bacon extra crispy since this lady has ordered all of the turkey parts," says Natasha Janine.

"Mari, can I get a glass of milk and a cup of tea? Virgie, I will determine which one I'm drinking after I get these details."

"Natasha Janine, girl you are too much."

Mari looks at Natasha Janine and asks, "Do you have a particular flavor of tea you would like to have ma'am?"

Saturday

Natasha Janine says, "I will take green tea."

Mari walks away from the table and I tell Natasha Janine, "Girl you are doing the most. I guess that's why we are friends." We both start laughing loudly.

My cell phone rings and to my surprise, it is Mr. Noble himself. I answer with my slow smiling sexy voice. Natasha Janine is looking at me with the side-eye. I roll my eyes and turn my lips up and start talking to my man like "take that."

"Hello, Mr. Noble! I'm out to breakfast with Natasha Janine at Kelle's. How are you this morning?" I love listening to him talk. I answer, "Yes, he is here, he is always here."

Noble is being nosey asking if Kelle's here. "I have on some sweatpants." I can't tell him I wore my red pants because he loves them too and for all the same reasons I do. "Ha ha, you know me too well," I knew he would know I wore them, but how he knows remains a mystery.

"We are about to eat so let me call you when we finish."

Noble just keeps talking and Natasha Janine is frowned up looking at me like "you so rude!"

"I decided to go to the office to work on some briefs for next week." He is not coming to my office; I wouldn't get anything completed.

"No, you cannot come to the office," I knew he would ask after I informed him of my plans. "You are too distracting, and I need to focus." He already knows this especially after what happened last night. I'm smiling too hard and say, "until we talk again, I will be thinking about you."

I looked over and Natasha Janine is staring at me frowned up and rolling her eyes too hard.

"What?" I say.

"I'm the one doing too much! Hell no! You are the one doing too much. Talking about until we talk again! Noble has you saying all type of shit."

I tell Natasha Janine to shut up! "Girl, you know that sounded cute as hell."

We laugh and she says, "It did, and I have to steal that one." I knew she would.

"Virg, tell me what happened I'm dying to know."

15

"Girl, okay where do I start?"

"From the beginning, dang!" She says with an attitude. I can see from the look on her face that she wants me to spill the tea.

So, I start talking. "Yesterday Noble called and said he wanted to come over. Girl, I told him I had work to do but he was persistent. He was focused on coming over and wasn't going to stop asking so I gave in. He was talking about how he was thinking of me and needed so badly to see me. Now, Natasha Janine, you know me. I'm in the house in a t-shirt and some sweatpants. Luckily, I had brushed my teeth, so my breath wasn't funky. At first, I was thinking I should put on some clothes because all he wants to do is just see me. Plus, it was raining and gloomy outside and you know what kind of mood that would put you in."

"The kind that makes you not want to be bothered," Natasha Janine is saying with her head down while biting her fingernail.

"I kept going back and forth on whether I should change my clothes or not. So, you already know, I changed my clothes, but I just put on one of those summer dresses we got from Italy.

"Which one heifer?" She asks impatiently and then says, "I already know which one you wore, but I want you to tell me."

"Natasha Janine, you don't know which one."

"I do know."

"Then you tell me, and I'll tell you if you are right."

"Girl you wore that black chiffon minidress and you wore it because it is an A-Line with a loose fit."

"I hate you. How did you know?"

"Virgie, I have been knowing you almost all my life, and to tell the truth that's the one I would have worn."

We give each other a high five and a "you know that's right," head tilt.

"Yep, I sure did, and you know I had to do my brows too. Say it with me, brows not done will never get you none."

We start laughing so hard that Kelle comes over to our table. He says, "You ladies are enjoying yourselves. It is a pleasure to see your smiling faces and hear your familiar voices. I have to ask what we did to deserve your patronage today?"

I said, "You know we love the food here that's it that's all."

"Well, thank you and we are open 7 days a week don't make your visits so far and in between. Carry on!"

Mari walks to the table and says, "Ladies, is everything okay over here I see the owner was over here? Your food should be here soon."

I told her, "No we know him personally and he was coming over to say hi."

She continues and asks, "Okay, do you need anything before your food comes?"

"Yes, can you make sure we have hot syrup, extra butter, napkins both wet and dry ones, thank you, please ma'am?" Mari leaves the table.

Natasha Janine says, "What happened yesterday? Girl tell me. This man Noble needs a brother, a cousin, or a friend that admires him enough to copy everything he does."

"Nope, I'm good on that. I love the fact that he is one of a kind."

Natasha is in agreement and says, "There is no lie in that part!"

Mari returns to the table again. "Virgie, Mr. Sid wanted me to tell you he made you something extra sweet and that he is so happy you are here. He said don't leave without him seeing you."

"Please tell him, I said I will make sure of it."

She hands the blueberry pancakes with the extra crispy bacon to Natasha Janine. Mari then hands me my banana pancakes which are shaped like a heart with bananas on top of it. Sid is the sweetest chef I know, and he makes you feel like you are the sweetest person he knows. I love me some him. Mari places the hot syrup, extra butter, and napkins on the table.

"Do you all need anything else?" We both reply "No!"

She then turns and walks away and says, "I will check back shortly and enjoy your meals."

"Okay thank you!"

Natasha Janine says, "Girl, why did Sid send you some heart-shaped pancakes. That old man knows he loves him some Virg."

"Girl, he is just nice and is especially nice to me." We both laughed and began to grub.

"Now, where did I leave off?"

17

"You were talking about what you had on."

"Oh yeah, so I had changed my clothes but was still working when he rang the doorbell. You know me, I played along. Who is it? Knowing dang well it was him because I never have company over. My home is a company free space."

"You know I know. I have to call, text, email, schedule an appointment with reminders just to stop by."

"Whatever!"

"So, what happened next?"

He said, "It's me, the only one you want to see."

I said, "Really how do you know?"

Girl he goes on to say, "I can tell by the smile you have on your face and I can't even see it, but I know it's there. If it's not true, I will leave but if it is true, you won't be disappointed."

So, I didn't open that door.

"What? Did he leave? I would have unlocked that door so fast he would have thought it had a sensor on it and sensed he was standing there and opened up."

"Girl, you know I opened that door, but not after I hesitated first. When I opened the door; he was standing right there."

"Was he? How did he look?"

"Simply magnificent! He must have just gotten a haircut because his lining lined his face perfectly. I was able to see the structure of his face like it was carved by the steadiest of hands delicately chiseled."

"Virgie, you better describe your man. Tell me more about his fine ass!"

"He had a white V-neck Pima cotton shirt on, fitted blue jeans, and those gray and white Jordan's. Girl, when I tell you he was looking great and not to mention his shirt was wet from walking in the rain from his car to my place. It made him glisten."

"You know I had to play tough so I told him "If you're wet you can't come in here." He said, "That is the whole reason I'm here." I asked, "What is?" He went on and said, "Let me show you." So, I walked away from the door and he followed me into the living room."

"Virgie shut the hell up now. You just wait one minute. This is tea worthy. No creamy white milk over here."

Saturday

Kelle has now returned to the table with his daughter Nuri. "Virgie, I told Nuri you were here, and she wanted to see you." Nuri is his four-year-old daughter, and she is so cute. She loves wearing a big Afro puff on the top of her head with deep dimples in her cheeks. I reach out my hands to give her a big hug and before I knew it, there's her mom Cheryl looking all crazy. Cheryl is Kelle's ex-wife, and she is so protective of him that it will make your head hurt.

Cheryl says to Nuri, "Enough of that hugging stuff. Say bye to your little friends because we have to go."

Nuri turns and runs towards her mom saying, "Bye-bye Ms. Virgie, I miss you!"

"Nuri baby, I miss you too! Since we are friends, maybe your mother will let us have a playdate with your dad like old times sake," I say while winking at Kelle as I talk.

Kelle interjects and says, "We would love that let me check my schedule and get back with you."

"Please do so, it's going to be great to be back together again."

Cheryl rolls her eyes and walks away with Nuri and Kelle following behind her.

Natasha Janine asks, "Why did you say that? You aren't going to play with that child."

"Girl, I know but since her mom wanted to throw shade, I pulled out my umbrella. You see that daddy loves him some Virgie and that drives her crazy. You see how quickly he responded smiling cheek to cheek. I'm all covered up over here so take that Cheryl with your mean ass."

"Girl, I have to admit I love that they are able to have such a functioning relationship with their daughter but all of those family events, vacations, and time they spend together is so overwhelming.

She can have it; she isn't wrong to be protective because Kelle is a great catch. I'm just not playing baseball in that field any longer."

We are still laughing at the look Cheryl had on her face when Natasha

Janine puts us back on the topic at hand.

19

"Girl, we have been here for about an hour and I'm going to need a mimosa now. Where is Mari, Mary, Missy whatever her name is?"

"She is over there. I will get her attention for you."

I get her attention by waving my napkin, but I get Kelle's attention too and he comes over with her. Natasha Janine starts talking to him instead. "Can I have a glass of mimosa?"

He says, "You all must really be gossiping that you need a real drink this early."

I don't know why he said that, but he knows this girl does not have a buffer.

"Kelle, you should continue to mind the business that pays you. An owner who tends to his customers' business is an owner who has no business. Now, may I have my drink?"

He says to her, "You haven't changed a bit which means you are still single and living your life through Virgie's life that is still quite sad. I will get your drink. Now continue enjoying your meal that has been comped by the owner of this fine establishment."

Kelle walks away shaking his head. When he was no longer in sight, I start laughing uncontrollably at both of them. They can't stand each other.

Natasha Janine says, "I can't stand Kelle's proper ass."

"And he can't stand yours either," I laugh.

She rolls her eyes and continue eating her pancakes, smacking her lips the whole time.

"Girl, let me finish telling you what happened."

"Yeah, please do because your ex-boyfriend got on my last damn nerve."

"Girl forget about him. I need your full attention. It's about to get good."

"Remember, I said I walked in the living room and he was behind me so I sat down in the chair which would force him to sit on the couch right?"

"Right, because he couldn't sit on your lap that would be goofy."

"Well, he didn't sit on the couch. He sat on the floor right in front of me rubbing my legs."

"What? What did you do or say?"

"I couldn't say anything. It felt so good that I became a ball of emotions inside bursting open like fireworks. I kept talking and typing on my laptop like I didn't feel his hands on my legs and feet."

"Are you hungry?" He asked.

I said, "A little, are you ordering or cooking?"

Girl he then said, "Baby what do you want? I came to see you but pleasing you will be upon your request."

He got up off the floor and stood in front of me and said, "What would you like?" I smiled and said, "I would like to have you cooking topless in the kitchen."

He was just standing up there smiling at me like he wanted me to request something else and said, "As you will have me."

I told you he says that whenever I tell him to do something or go somewhere.

Noble always says "I will do it as you will have me to do it."

He took that shirt off so fast and got to cooking, you hear me got to cooking, I had to say that again. He was bending over to get the pots from the cabinet, reaching up on the shelf grabbing dishes, standing in the doorway of the refrigerator taking food out. I stopped typing so I would not miss a beat, I felt like it was a big strip tease performance and I mean he performed. What the hell? This man drives me crazy!

"Damn, then what happened but wait till they bring my drink. I'm going to need my own carafe of mimosa. This man be doing too much, but I love every bit of it, and I know you do Virgie. With his fine ass. When we met him at the concert, I should have introduced myself to him when I saw him, but no! My ass was drinking so much beer that I had to go piss."

"You always talk about that like he was trying to talk to you. You asked him, where was the restroom and he showed you. I am the one who asked him if he saw where you went and started talking to him while I waited on you. Girl bye! You kill me with that."

"Virgie, I still saw him first."

"Oh ok, and how did that work out for you?"

"Girl, finish telling the damn story."

"I would if you wouldn't keep interrupting me."

Mari returns to the table with a carafe of mimosa and two glasses. I thank her and then grab me a glass. I need to calm down if I am going to finish. This lady knows how to change a mood like flipping a switch. But I love her crazy ass.

"Like I was saying, he was over there cooking topless and flexing his muscles. Girl, I couldn't take my eyes off him. He was boiling water for the cauliflower rice. And, you should have seen the steam flowing up his body as he stood over that stove. That chocolate-colored skin was shining like copper metal does after being polished. I was able to see every curve of those muscles too. I was in a trance captivated by his every move. He turned and said something, but I had checked out of my physical body and was engrossed with the thoughts in my mind. Next thing I know, he walked over to where I was still sitting and handed me a plate of cauliflower rice, sautéed chicken breast, garlic bread, and a glass of Merlot. He handed me the plate and leaned in and kissed me. It was not just any kiss, but you know the wet passionate kiss like 'I haven't seen you in ages and you need to taste how much I miss you' kind of kiss.

"Girl stop playing. He did that. Wow, tell me more."

"I quickly lost my appetite, but it looked so good I began eating it anyway."

"I asked him, "Are you going to eat?"

He said, "I ate before I came over. I told you I came to see you, and that's what I wanted to do."

So, I said, "Well you have seen me, cooked for me, and are now driving me crazy. Are you leaving now?"

He said, "Do you want me to leave?" As he stood there biting his bottom lip.

I told him, "No I am really enjoying your company."

He then walked over to the balcony door and put his shirt back on and said, "It is raining pretty hard and the word that comes to mind is the one you said when I arrived."

I asked him, "What word is that?"

Girl he said, "Wet! You know you said it when I was standing at the door."

I told him, "Yeah I remember."

He then said to me, "Come and let's play on that word before I leave. Wet! Virgie, come stand with me on the balcony in this rain."

"So, I let him guide me onto the balcony in the early morning hours of dawn. Girl, he was standing there in those jeans behind me as I gripped the rail tightly like I had the strength to snatch it off. We were out in the rain letting each drop pound on our bodies like it was a sunny day and we were standing soaking up the vitamin D. He held me from the back so I could feel his excitement from being so close to my body! He moved his hands from my thighs slowly up to my breast and began caressing them, you know he calls these breast pillows. He was gently moving back and forth from breast to my legs rubbing them softly then aggressively on the outside of my legs moving to the inside. Then to my thighs while keeping his hand under my dress pressing me closer to his body. We were soaking wet all over from the rain and girl, this passion we shared was so intense."

He said, "Remember that word wet as he whispered in my ear."

"Yes, I do!" I said as I was breathing all heavily.

Girl he asked me, "Are you ready to be wet?"

At that time, I was ready, so I said, "Yes!" And I had to grapple with that word. I couldn't even grab a hold of my breath. I felt like the rain was sucking the air right out of my body. He then slid the back of my dress up and never even gave any indication of being surprised that I didn't have on any panties. It was as if he knew I wouldn't. Girl, this man was too much."

"Virgie, tell the story. This is a hot sauna of stories."

"Okay, next thing he did was whisper in my ear, hold on tight and know that I got you."

He pulled out a wrapper from his pocket and tore it open with his teeth. He slowly unfastened his jeans to tease me because he knew I was ready and soaked from the rain among other things. He then pulled his briefs down and bent my torso slightly over the rail so that I could grip the rail tighter.

He whispered, "Don't let go" and asked me to promise. "Girl, you know I said with the quickness that I promise. I was so anxious for the next moment, but he did nothing. Just held me there and he just kept kissing me softly on my neck, on the sides, the back, and biting my shoulders. So, I waited for him to enter my cherished space."

"Virgie, you know I don't know all those damn terms he gave you. Please just say the words for your anatomy."

"Girl be quiet. The words are what makes it work for me. Let me give you a refresher course on his words for my anatomy so you can understand why it works for me. My breasts are pillows, my legs are long stems of my body's extension, my neck is a branch, this vagina is a sweet muscle, and my derrière is my cushion. And, before you ask me, yes, he has names for his anatomy too. His penis is his strong muscle, and his fingers are instruments. I hope you are caught up so I can finish telling you what happened, dang!" Look at her writing this stuff down; she doesn't miss a beat. I love this lady!

Now, I will finish telling you, "Girl, Noble finally made his entrance known and I felt all of it. He was moving with the pace of the rain and when the rain picked up so did, he. Girl, it was as if he had talked to the rain gods and they moved to the same beat of his drums. I couldn't see a thing, but I felt every muscle in his body while he was still holding me. And then I felt the force of his nature and I erupted. He continued whispering in my ear "wet" while meeting me with every stroke of passion, with every push, and with every pound of rain landing on my body. I began clenching my muscles tighter and tighter. He said it again "wet" slowly to place an emphasis on every symbol of the word. We were on that balcony in that rainstorm, in the heat of the night, and I released myself exploding like this was my first time."

He yelled loudly "I love it, I love it!" and I grapple with the words "I love it too!"

"Virgie, all I can say is damn, damn, and damn!"

It is always a good time when I get together with Natasha Janine. She knows how to pump me up especially when I'm sharing something that is so personal. I love eating at Kelle's. The restaurant has an aura that is inviting and is the ultimate social hub. I have to say that Kelle looks great too, but I dare not tell him that. He would set up camp outside my home like he was on a stakeout waiting for the right moment to move in. And, to believe Cheryl tried to come for me when she knows that I don't want Kelle is baffling. She should be happy she is still able to eat from the payments my friends and I make at that restaurant. I send mad crowds of people over there. If anything, she should be thanking me that her man is still in business. Enough about these two people, let me get to the office to work on these briefs. I hope traffic isn't crazy, but I do live in Chicago and today is Saturday so I may be stuck in traffic for hours.

Ring, ring, ring, it's my Aunt. I answer because she will keep calling until you do. "Hey, auntie, what's up? Wait one minute so I can connect you to my car. Okay, you connected, what's up?"

"Hey Niecy, I was wondering if you have a couple of dollars?"

"Yeah, I do, what do you need?"

"Your Auntie wants to go to dinner with these old bitches and I'm short about $40."

"No problem I will send it when I stop driving." I give this lady whatever she wants. "Auntie, what have you been up to because I haven't heard from you in a couple of days?"

"Niecy, now you know me, and this man is still getting it on. I told him he has to stop working me out like that because I'm sleeping in my bed like I'm a fucking cowgirl and this ben-gay isn't working like it used too."

I start laughing so hard. "Auntie, why are you telling me this? You know I can't take it hearing these stories from you."

"Shit Virgie Mae, you are the only person I can tell. You know when you are telling your business to these bitches, they are plotting to try to take your spot. I know damn well you don't want this old ass man. Shit, I don't want this old ass man either, but this man treats me so nice I can't imagine someone else reaping these benefits and that sex is great, hell. I'm not getting any younger. How about you? Are you finally getting some sex because that thing is going to dry up and ain't nobody going to want it? I know because I have several girlfriends who have had that shit happen to them. They're around here looking like prunes."

"Auntie, how do you know?"

"You can tell by their faces. They are always scrunched up like they smell something. When I see these bitches around here frowned up like they smell something I say, "bitch it's you that you smell, it's you bitch!" We both laugh so hard.

"Auntie, I'm at the office when I get settled, I will send it. I love you and have a good time."

"I will Niecy and thank you."

This is my favorite aunt. She has no filter and says exactly what she wants to say. She told me, "When you have lived as long as I have, I say fuck trying to have people like you, or seek approval for the things you are doing in your life, or trying to impress a motherfucker, fuck them!" But she is only 65 years old, and she swears she is so old, so I say, "Oh okay tell them how you feel then." You can't tell her nothing, she is too funny.

I pull into the garage and notice that it is quite empty. Here I am on my off day "working for wages." I forgot all about how I was supposed to be taking it easy. Let me get out of this car so I don't spend my whole day in this building. I feel my phone vibrating but where is it? Here it is in my bag. "Hello! Let me put on my earpiece. I'm walking into the office now." It's Natasha Janine calling me.

"I did have a great time; you know you are crazy, but I love you. Bye girl! I'm going to get into this office and watch I be here all day."

When I arrived at my office, I looked at my phone and realized my older sister called me last night and I forgot to return her call. I immediately dialed her number and she answered on the second ring.

"Hello MJ, you called me last night? I was talking with Noble. He came over. You don't know what we were doing?"

My sister MJ is the saint in our family. I mean that for real. I can't tell her anything about what really happens when Noble and I get together.

I say, "He made dinner and we talked then he left." I keep it short and to the point.

I continue saying, "I'm in the office. I will have to call you later. Love ya."

MJ can't handle the details of my moments. If she knew we were on the balcony in the rain doing what we were doing, she would be drenching me in her bless oil and have me looking like a fried golden-brown chicken. She would say, "Virgie Mae, there is no sex before marriage," and especially after what happened with me and Kelle definitely proves she isn't wrong. Although Noble and I are adults we understand that our actions have consequences, so some things are safe and better left unsaid, even by my sister MJ.

While I am turning on my computer my office line is ringing. Mr. Noble is calling me. He thinks he is coming to my office. Nope, he does not even have a chance of pulling that off. So, I answer it to let him down gently when he asks again.

"Hello Mr. Noble, how can I help you, and please know I got you on the speakerphone?"

"Ms. Virgie, do you think that I would refrain from saying the things I will say because you decided to take this risk."

"Knowing you, nope but I just thought I would share."

"Are you in the office alone?"

"Yes, I am, why are you asking?"

"I wanted to see how you are this afternoon, and I am curious to know if I aim to please yesterday?"

"Well, I'm fed, in great spirits, looking great, and feeling wonderful."

"Lady, you are messing with my mind because I can think of so many ways, I can play with you and the words you have chosen."

"Really Mr. Noble, make me a believer."

"Can I come to visit you in the office?"

"No, you cannot Mr. Noble. Help my mind receive what your hands and body want to do to me since you are so insistent to come to see me.

Can you do that?"

"I see there is another "as you have me" request I will have to grant. I am going to need you to close your office door but keep me on the speaker. I want my words to permeate the walls of that room."

"Okay, I'm closing the door and sitting at my desk."

Noble starts talking before my feet are planted on the floor. "Ms. Virgie, I would like to describe this "feeling" I have. It is the "feeling" that makes me move in pure delight about the time we shared last night. This "feeling" keeps my muscle strong, tight and at attention from the thought of being on the balcony soaking wet. It makes this normally stubborn muscle pulsate when my mind takes me back to that place. This "feeling" gives me this indescribable tightness in my pants, the involuntary shiver of my leg, not to mention this throbbing pain because it longs to be placed between your soft pillows. This "feeling" has me willing to risk my gym schedule with my guys because my hands want so badly to touch you. The "feeling" I have wants to sit you on top of that desk knocking everything over, laying you down on that wood so that you are properly positioned to receive this wood, keeping those blinds slightly open so the sun can pierce your skin, all the while I rub underneath your chin across the stem that holds your head unto your chest. This "feeling" has me wanting to break all the rules giving you more and more and more of me. This "feeling" I have wants to kneel down on the floor pulling your body to the edge of that desk and allowing my face to take shelter in your hidden place licking, sucking, and biting you oh so. Do you get how I'm feeling?"

"Yes, I do!" I say slowly and sensually since I'm now all hot and bothered.

"Then Ms. Lady, don't stay there all day. I have a real "feeling" you will need something to tie you over a little later. Until we talk again, I will be thinking about this feeling. Bye, my lady!"

"Bye!"

This man makes every muscle ache in my body and I was literally worn out. Now how am I supposed to work after he tells me about his "feeling?"

Why does this man do this to me? I remember when I met Noble. We were at a concert for this local artist listening to some reggae music. Natasha Janine and I was having the time of our lives when she drank so many beers that she kept running to the restroom. It was some time after 10 pm, she left going to the restroom, but I was talking to a guy we had met and didn't see her leave. I was worried someone took her somewhere because she was so drunk. I stopped Noble in the hall and asked him if he had seen her or if he knew the direction she may have gone. I was asking him questions so fast that I didn't even notice how attractive he was. He asked me to calm down and that my friend went into the restroom down the hall. I turned to walk away so frantically I guess that's why he said, "Ma'am I'm coming with you to make sure she is okay."

I initially thought it was a good idea for him to come along with me. But then I began thinking what if he was a man who was trying to do something to her and now me because you can never know. I was so worried that I just went along with him coming with me in case there was another guy there bothering her. We have been out drinking before and some guys thought we were their girls since they just bought us some drinks.

Noble continued to tell me how she stopped him and didn't know where the restroom was, so he then pointed it out down the hall. Before I could leave to find her; he grabbed my hand to lead me down the hall. His hands were so soft that I remember commenting on them. He looked at me and said, "Thank you and your hands are quite soft too."

It was at that moment I saw the most beautiful, athletic, tall, dark, strong, well-dressed man of my dreams. When we got to the restroom entrance Natasha Janine was coming out. I walked up to her to make sure she was good and thanked him again for his help.

He said, "I know this may be a strange request, but can I give you a hug. I feel so bad that I have you, all, worried since I sent her to the restroom by herself." I said, "Sure!" He stretched his arms out and I walked in to give him a hug. He felt so good. He smelled just so delightful. I found myself holding on to him and to my surprise he didn't let me go. We stood there hugging in the middle of that hall like forever. And the best part of our relationship is that he has been holding me like that for the past 4 months. Never letting me go.

Enough reminiscing about Noble. I need to get started on these briefs. I started "working for wages." I am typing, writing, copying, filing, returning calls, and everything. It felt like I was only there a couple of hours but when I finally glanced at the clock, I had been here working for four straight hours. Let me call Noble, damn no answer. I then called Natasha Janine and she answered on the first ring.

"Girl, what are you doing?"

"Virgie, I am just sitting here listening to some cuts and drinking wine."

"I hear other voices, who do you have over there with you?"

"Twaab came by."

Twaab is my crazy little sister.

"Let me speak to her."

Twaab says, "What's happening Captain?"

"I called you yesterday. Why didn't you answer?" I asked her.

"Sister, I was busy, but you should have left me a message."

"Twaab, busy doing what?"

"Sister if I tell you, you aren't going to believe it."

"Then don't tell me. How long have you been over there?"

"Sister, why are you questioning me? I feel like I'm sitting on the witness stand testifying."

"Because I have to watch you with both eyes open."

"Sister, you aren't wrong, but watching me with both eyes open you still will be bound to miss something because there is no telling what I would be doing."

"My line is clicking and it's my Noble. Bye, lady."

"Wow sister, you drop everything for that man with his sweet ass and I mean that figuratively and literally. Bye, love you."

"I love you too."

Everyone in my family always says, "figuratively and literally" because we feel we have to emphasize when we are making a point.

Noble is calling my office I answer saying, "Hello, Mr. Noble!"

"Hey baby, why are you still in the office?"

"I just finished and was starting to head home."

"You want me to come over?"

"Noble, after last night, this morning, afternoon, and evening I would not be good company."

"Babe, don't say that, don't say that. You will always be the only company I will need. You want me to come and get you since you are so tired? I can bring you over here."

"No, you don't have to do that."

"If you want me to then I will."

"Yes, that would be great! I will leave my car in the garage."

"I was on my way there anyway when I saw I missed your call. I thought something was wrong, so I was coming to the rescue."

"Aww, thank you, babe. See you in a few. I will be in the lobby waiting."

This man, this man! I need to go brush my teeth and wash between my legs. I have been sitting here for hours. I know I'm sweating in all the wrong places. Let me hurry up because if he was on his way knowing him, he is already downstairs. He makes me smile too hard.

When I get downstairs in the lobby, I see he is here already. Noble gets out of his truck to escort me. He gives me a hug like the first time we met "never letting me go" then kisses me, sucking on my bottom lip. That is definitely his thang, he always does that, and I love it too. He is so sweet as my sister said. Twaab, my middle sister thinks Noble isn't really into women because of how he acts, how touchy, and soft he is. I keep trying to tell her that he is definitely into women more than she could ever imagine. Twaab's problem is that she is just not into men "Ha ha." Noble looks over at me and smiles.

"What are you smiling about?"

"I'm smiling because I'm so happy to be your driver, Ms. Lady."

"Well, push the pedal to the metal because Ms. Lady is tired."

"Wow, Ms. Lady is quite demanding."

We had to laugh at that while he rubs my hand as he drives to his condo. I love riding with him.

We pull up to his building and he greets the guard at the gate. I've never seen him before. Is he new?" I ask.

"Yes, he is a cool kid who has only been working here for a couple of weeks."

"Has it been that long since I been over here? Wow! I have to come to visit you more often."

"Virgie, why don't you move in?"

"Noble, what?"

"Yes, we would be able to see each other every day, your office is five minutes away, and I can drive my Lady everywhere she wants to go while she smiles the whole time. Tell me you will think about it."

He leans in close to my face and says, "Tell me please," then kisses my lips.

"Noble, I will think about it," is what I'm saying to him, but the truth is I know I am not going to be thinking it at all. I'm not thinking about it. I need my own space, place, and escape from everything in this world periodically. I love his condo, but I love being by myself even more. He opens the door to let me out of the truck reaching his hands out for my bag and purse. Noble doesn't let me carry anything. He would probably carry me if he could do it while holding my bag and purse. This man, this man.

Noble opens the door to his condo and I immediately notice the sweet smell of roses. He loves to have fresh flowers in his place. I don't care for flowers at all. I know it sounds odd, but I like looking at them, but I don't need them. He can't live without them.

"Virgie, would you like to shower or be bathed?"

"Be bathed? What does that mean?"

"You know what it means so which will it be?"

"I want to say to be bathed, but it will lead to so much more and to be perfectly honest I am really tired. I will shower but give me a rain check on the being bathed offer."

"There will be no rain checks for services offered today. "Enjoy your shower," he says with a seductive smirk on his face.

I made sure I was switching all seductively as I walked to the bedroom for my shower. I have clothes at his place. He wouldn't have it any other way. Noble makes sure they are laundered every week whether I come over or not. He has this thing about the smell of freshly laundered clothes. I don't understand it but again that's why I have to stay at my own place.

Saturday

When you live with someone, you will be expected to follow the rules or requests of the other person. I do what I want in my house when, how, and wherever I want. As Twaab would say, "You are not wrong, and believe me she is definitely right."

This shower is a dream shower. There are three different shower heads with jet speeds and a smart television embedded in the wall here. I love to hear music when I shower over here. When I'm home I have to settle for the one shower head and the okay jet speed. I walk out of the shower wrapped in a towel and Noble walks into the room. He looks at me and says, "You tired right?"

I smile and say, "Yes I am."

He shakes his head and walks out of the room. Noble loves for a woman to wear silk gowns to bed so there can be a lot of slipping and sliding in the bed. He makes sure I have a supply of them at his place. I recall asking him why and he said, "Only the softest material should touch a woman's body when she sleeps so her man's hand can easily slide under it." I used to wonder, was this man full of shit, or does he really feel that way? I learned quickly that he feels exactly how he speaks. I walk into the kitchen and he is preparing himself a sandwich.

"We're eating sandwiches this late," I ask.

"We?" as if he is asking a question.

"Yes, we! I know I smelled something being cooked in here and I know it wasn't a sandwich."

"I thought you were so tired. I didn't think you would be hungry at this time of night."

"Noble, it's only 9:45 p.m. What are you talking about?"

"Every time I am about to ask you something you have pointed out you're tired, so I dare not interfere with your request to be left alone."

"Aww, Mr. Noble is feeling like he is not needed. I guess I will order UberEATS since I'm hungry and have no desire to eat a sandwich.

Where is my phone?"

Noble runs to the bedroom and grabs my phone. "You are so stubborn I guess that's why you are a good attorney."

33

"No, the reason I'm a good attorney is because I'm smart, tenacious, hardworking, and get the job done. Now, what did you make for me to eat?"

He leans in and kisses me taking my lips into his mouth. The wetness of his tongue makes me open my mouth to give him the same level of passion he gives. Noble pulls me close, rubbing his hand alongside my body. He kisses my left cheek, then begins sucking my jaw, biting my earlobe, kissing my stem (the name he has given for my neck) all the while rubbing his hands on my body. I put on a t-shirt and shorts as sleepwear so he would know I was tired. Noble didn't care. He was rubbing his hands all over me. You would think I had on a silk gown how smoothly his hands were sliding up and down my body. While he is sucking and kissing my neck, Noble grabs the waist of my shorts and slides his hand between my legs rubbing the top of my vagina.

"Noble, touch me, touch me please."

He whispers, "But you're so tired."

"Then give me energy!" I sternly express what I need him to do.

And then he perfectly enters his finger into my place moving it in and out, in and out, slow then fast. Right, when I am about to release, he pulls it out and whispers, "This one instrument will not do it" and he puts two fingers in now moving them both in and out and in and out until I finally release everything I had been holding inside.

SUNDAY

Now I'm up and I've realized that I didn't eat anything last night. I'm starving and Noble has me smothered underneath him. I have to get something to eat. But first, I have to make my great escape because if he feels me move, I will be trapped here forever. I love me some him, but I need to get out of this bed. What did he cook last night that smelled so good? I bet he put it in the refrigerator. As I grab the handle, Noble says, "I ate it last night. I know what you are looking for and it was shrimp scampi in an olive oil garlic sauce with angel hair pasta noodles."

"Really Noble, you couldn't save some for me? So, I know you are taking me out for breakfast because I'm hungry and to be really honest I'm hungry now."

"Virgie, I ordered breakfast to be delivered. I enjoy being in the house with you, so I didn't want us to leave. It should be here shortly. Are you showering or bathing?"

"Noble, don't even try it I'm lying back down," as I walk back to the bedroom to get back in bed and he moves out of the doorway.

"Excuse me, Ms. Lady!"

I laugh because again I am hangry.

It was shortly after that his phone rang from the front desk. Noble tells me the delivery is here.

"Do you want to be served in bed or are you coming into the kitchen?"

"I'm coming into the kitchen."

As hungry as I am, I don't have any time to be watching if I spilled something on these sheets. I hear him open the door and thank someone. I get up and he is setting up the table for us to eat.

"Do you need some help?"

"No Ms. Lady, you rest, and I will be finished shortly."

I laugh and smile while he was scurrying around the kitchen. Noble hates paper plates so the food has to be served on china. I think it has something to do with his past, but he has never said it.

35

He ordered from Kelle's; I pray that Kelle himself didn't bring it. Kelle sometimes does the deliveries for the restaurant because he likes to employ people and do all of their work.

Noble says, "I ordered from your spot, and no your ex-boyfriend didn't deliver the food."

"How do you know? You don't even know him?"

"Ms. Lady, I don't know him, but please know I've met the man before and I would never forget a face."

"You met who?"

"Kelle, that's who."

"Why is this the first time I'm hearing this?"

"You have never asked."

"I didn't ask you this time either."

"Well, your eyes asked so I shared."

"So now you are an eye reader?"

"Really Virgie, it's an optometrist? You are really different when you wake up, eye reader."

He laughs so hard he almost drops the plate.

I'm very curious about his visit to Kelle's. Kelle's is my favorite breakfast restaurant.

But, right now let me get back to Mr. Noble.

"Noble, I'm waiting to hear about this visit to the restaurant my ex-boyfriend owns when you don't even like eating breakfast, especially pancakes."

"Virgie, it was about a month ago, Raq and I were out golfing, and he suggested we stop at this restaurant because he heard the food was good."

Raq is Noble's best friend. He is also tall, handsome, athletic, and funny as hell. His only problem is he is a hoe. And I mean hoe's hoe. I mean a nasty hoe, trifling, a dirty dog hoe.

Noble goes on to say, "I asked him what's the name of the place and he said Kelle's. I remember you told me that you love the food there. This was after you told me he was your ex. So of course, I was interested in going. When we pulled up, I wasn't really impressed by the location of the restaurant or the look of the establishment. It was small and appeared dirty from the outside.

Sunday

There was a long line. The hostess was rude. She said, "How many," while holding her head down with a very dry tone of voice. She never even made eye contact with us. She then said with the same tone, "I know you see how many people out here waiting. So, you will definitely be waiting before I can get you a table."

I know exactly the hostess he's talking about...my youngest sister Dominica. I let him continue. I need to get to the details first.

Noble then says, "I asked Raq why we would support this establishment with this kind of customer service. He said the same reason we support others. So, we waited the hour or so it took to get a table. Finally, this guy came out and apologized for the wait. He promised everyone 15% discount off the bill. He introduced himself as Kelle, the sole owner of the restaurant. I could not forget him. I experienced an owner caring enough to put the customers before his profits."

"Noble, what did you think when you got inside the restaurant?"

"I thought never to judge a restaurant by the entrance. I enjoyed the food, the service inside was great, and the ambiance was perfect. Kelle knows what he is doing because changing the mood of the customers by giving us a discount for the wait actually eased the tempers of the people.

He came over to each table and thanked everyone personally for waiting. Kelle seemed like a cool dude, but you know Raq was trying to get some extras, but that dude Kelle was not budging."

"Well, I'm glad you had a great time. The hostess you met was my little sister Dominica."

"What? Really!" He asks like he is in a state of shock.

"So, she works there? Wow! She was so rude. Cute lady but definitely rude.

"Dominica used to work there."

"Virgie did she get fired?" He says as if he is not surprise by this information.

S. S. Suggs

"Yeah, but not for the way she talked to customers. She overslept and didn't show up to work after three or four times. Kelle had to let her go."

"Why haven't I ever met her?"

"I don't know but she's a sweet person just a little rough especially when her feet hurt, and she is tired." We both start laughing.

"I will make that happen very soon; you will like her crazy ass."

"Thanks, I want to meet everyone in your family. They will soon be my family too."

"We're getting married. Was I asleep when you proposed? Did I say yes, and I can't remember?

Did you slip me some narcotics when we were kissing?"

"Okay, Ms. Lady I see you have jokes. You know you can have this every day of your life," he said while taking his hands swiping up and down his body.

"Are you finished eating Ms. Lady so I may clean off the table?"

"Yes, I am."

Then I hand him my plate, Noble walks to the counter and says, "I have a taste for something sweet."

I say, "Those pancakes were extremely sweet."

"Yeah, I know, but I would love to taste your sweetness."

He then walks over to me, picks me up, carries me to the bedroom, then lays me on the bed. He stood there glaring at me and I immediately begin acting all bashful and tried to scurry away. I then turn my head so he can't see my face.

"Virgie, why do you do that?"

"Do what?"

"You know, become uncomfortable with me staring at you."

"I don't know. I didn't realize I was doing that."

"Virgie, you are simply beautiful, and I love watching what God has made. I watch everything you do, and you do it, the Virgie way. Babe, you can walk into a room and own every step, but if I turn the lights on you shy away. There is nothing about you, your body, or your smile that would make me not love who you are."

He is right for some reason I think of my imperfections instead of basking in my moment of his admiration for me. I am smiling so hard which makes my jaws hurt after hearing how he sees me.

"Thank you for sharing Mr. Noble."

My cell phone rings. I turn on my stomach to get it and answer it but forgot about what we were about to do. Noble grabs hold of my long branches of extension of my lower body and pulls me down to the edge of the bed while I'm on my stomach.

Noble says, "I have a request and I need it fulfilled but you Ms. Lady has chosen the direction in which it's given and taps me on my derrière."

"What's happening here?"

Noble pulls down my shorts and starts kissing my cushion as he calls my butt. First softly, slowly, then adding some wetness to it.

"I never get enough of you. I want to do things with this tongue that surprises and excites you all at the same times."

Noble continues to say, "These cushions have to be separated so I can tend to them one at a time."

This man and the names that he gives these body parts drives me insane, but I love every one of them. He touches them then squeezes them before he spreads them apart.

He says, "I love the smell of your body, it drives me wild."

Next thing I know, I'm releasing after the first touch of his tongue against my opening. I'm wiggling from excitement, but he does not stop. He picks up speed then places his arms underneath my long extensions and lifts me up. He makes every muscle in my body ache from this arousing pleasure and he is doing it without any signs of ceasing. He keeps going and going and going then he stops and enters his finger in that butt opening to finish me off. He went in and out moving it back and forth then in and out and back and forth.

I release, "please I can't please this is too intense," then I am at a loss for my words.

He sped up this assault of pleasure and then asked, "Have you reached your max?" And crazy me says "No" trying to be tough. I can handle it. I'm a grown woman. How dare he ask me a question like that? I knew damn well I was finished before we

39

started. I have to get some vitamins. I'm over here thinking my thoughts I then feel a thrusting motion. There are two, two fingers he has up in there and it was over for me. If this man doesn't stop it with this, I'm going to work from his condo for the rest of my life. We are going outside. We will not do this all day and night.

At this moment, I'm realizing I did fall asleep. Now I'm up wondering how I'm in this bed with just a T-shirt on. I remember now looking over at Noble sleeping on the other side of the bed. This man wears himself out. I always wonder has he always been like this and if so, why is he single and not married? Noble told me that it's been almost three and a half years since his last relationship. He asked me to never ask about that relationship if I am enjoying the relationship, we have. I respect his request, but I do often wonder what happened. Whatever happened he dare not relive it nor discuss it. I am in deep thought and I see that Noble is awake.

"Virgie, how long have you been up?" As he tries to gather himself.

"I just got up!" I was up thinking for a while.

"Are you hungry?" I see this look on my face didn't reveal how I feel. "Yes, Noble let's go outside." We could definitely use some human interaction outside of these walls.

"Are you sure because we can stay in if you want and watch a movie? I promise I will be good. I shouldn't promise because you will make a liar out of me in a matter of minutes. Let's shower and get going. The sooner we get out the sooner we can get back. I have a word I would like to play on. It has been on my mind and I know you will love it."

A word? What word? I hope he is not trying to propose because he was just talking about having me move in, my family will be his family, and meeting my crazy sister. I hate it when he does this.

Now I am going to be thinking about this all day, analyzing everything he says and does, and acting all nervous. You know what? I will not let him do that to me today.

"Noble! Baby, what do you mean by you have a word you want to play on?"

Sunday

"Virgie, you know how I get a word in my head and use our intimate time to perform our own soliloquy. You know it's our own Chocolate Soliloquy that we share together while I discover the pleasures of your desires."

Noble with his own play on a word. Soliloquies are his thing, and everyone has a thing. He is in touch with all of his senses. Noble is what I would call a sensual lover.

"Oh, okay Noble?"

"What did you think I was talking about?"

"I thought you were trying to ask me to marry you," I say and start giggling because I feel embarrassed.

"In due time Virgie, I already know I want to spend the rest of my life with you, but you are not ready, and I understand that completely so I will wait. And while I wait, I will make the most of every moment we have together. Since we are talking about my word...It is moment."

"Noble maybe we should stay in?" Before he can answer I then say, "I'm just playing I need some fresh air."

It is so nice out today. I love Chicago in the summertime especially downtown. Noble lives down here which is perfect for me since I love walking. I could walk everywhere down here if it was up to me, but he is always sold on taking some form of transportation.

"Noble, can we walk along the river?"

"Is that what you want to do?"

"Yeah, let's walk, get some wine, sit out here, and watch the people on boats. I know you would like to go shopping but this idea is cheaper."

"Virgie, you know I'm on a fixed income."

"As much as you shop, I would never even imagine that."

"I love nice things and I am not afraid to buy what I want."

"If anyone is on a fixed income, I think it's me because it pains me to spend money."

"Virgie, you don't have to spend money. I can give you whatever you need, and you can spend all of my money."

"Noble, that's sweet of you to offer, but the last time I checked you are not currently employed."

"But that doesn't mean I don't have money."

"Remember, how you say, "work for wages" I just stopped working."

"Alrighty, Mr. Noble, the big spender. Since you have so much money, I would like to go on a boat ride."

"I will call and tell him to bring my boat out just for you."

I started laughing. He doesn't have a boat and he know he doesn't. I turned away so that I would not laugh in his face for being so arrogant then I noticed he pulls out his phone and dials a number for real. I wonder, who is he calling about this request?

I hear him say, "Bring the boat to the dock on Wacker and State, take your time, telephone me when you are close, and I will see you soon."

I ask immediately, "Who was that?"

"That is a young man who takes care of my boat."

"I didn't know you had a boat."

"Virgie, yes I have a boat amongst other things. I have a little of this and a little of that but I'm not bragging."

"Okay Mr. Noble, let's get some wine and wait for our ride on your little paddle boat." I knew when I said it that he was going to put me to shame. Nothing he does is little, and he definitely wouldn't have made a call for a little paddle boat to show up. We could have just gone on a boat tour instead.

We are sitting on a bench on the side of the dock when we see several boats pull up to the dock.

People are getting on and off of boats in bathing suits. Old, young, white, black, Asians, and Latinos riding on boats in small or large groups. We are waiting for Mr. Noble's boat when his phone starts ringing. He answers it and says, "We are right here, do you see me? I'm waving my hand," while waving his hand in the air. I look to see who he is waving at and a young man who slightly resembles Noble starts waving back and forth smiling. This young man is handsome with a low haircut with waves like the ocean. He appears to be tall, medium build, and looks athletic too.

I say to Noble, "Who is that?"

He says, "That's the young man who takes care of my boat for me, come let's get on it."

Sunday

When I say it wasn't a little paddle boat, it is a yacht if you ask me, but I don't know anything about boats. I have been on a couple of boat trips, but this right here beats all of those. It is immaculate in every way. It was as if the young man knew Noble would call him and he had it cleaned just for us.

Noble says, "Hey Daryl I'm so happy you weren't busy and is able to accommodate my baby's request."

"Noble it's your boat so whenever or wherever you need it, it's my job to bring it. Hello ma'am."

"Excuse my rudeness Daryl, this is the lady of my life Virgie. Virgie, this is Daryl, my only son."

Son? I didn't know he had children and not to mention a grown ass son who he refers to as "the young man who takes care of my boat." Hell naw, this shit is about to be over before it starts.

Son? Noble interrupts me, caught up in my thoughts.

"Virgie, Daryl isn't my real son, but I have cared for him all of his life as if he is. Isn't that correct Daryl?"

Daryl replies, "Yes Sir, Noble has looked after me better than my own parents. I owe him my life."

Wow, here I go, going off in my head before I even hear the whole story.

"It is very nice to meet you Daryl and it appears that you have been taking great care of this fine vessel," I say as I climb aboard.

Daryl asks Noble, "Do you want me to steer the boat while you all relax?"

"Yes, thank you."

"I know this sweet woman here and she has a thousand questions so I will give her my undivided attention."

He knows me too well. Because I need answers. What does this young man mean by saying "better than my parents" about Noble? Is he the ex-girlfriend's son? Or is he really his real son and the mother hasn't told him yet? Is he adopted? Noble grabs my hand and leads me down under the deck of the boat. It is spacious down here with a small bar, restroom, and full-size bed. I sit at the bar and he immediately start talking.

"Daryl is my friend's son that he had with a one-night stand. My friend who I care not to mention by name was not in a position financially to assist the mother. I felt pretty bad for the situation at hand, and I started giving my friend money to care for his child. This friend of mine decided after several years of supporting his son that he would take a paternity test to confirm if the boy was, indeed, his child after he came into a position of wealth. Let me say that the paternity test revealed that he wasn't the father at which time he ceased all assistance. Daryl was coming of age. My friend and I had shown Daryl what it meant to have a village take care of him. So, I suggested to my friend that he continue to support him regardless of the results of the test because he was the only father the boy had known. He adamantly refused. It was hurting my heart that the child we were basically teaching to be a black man in this world would be forced to depend solely on his mother. His mother really did "work for wages" if you know what I mean.

So, long story short I made it my responsibility to teach, guide, fund, and support this young man in everything he does. To answer all your other questions, I am not the friend, don't ask me who the friend is, and no I have not made this story up to make myself look like an angel. Now, can we enjoy this boat ride. Oh yeah, I forgot about this answer to a question you may ask. I never slept or paid for the services of his mother either ma'am."

"Well, thank you for sharing, and don't be surprised later if I have more questions," I say while I give him the pouty lips and rolling my eyes. "If I know you, Virgie, who I do, I will be on the witness stand before this trip is over, I'm sure of it."

"Well, it is your idea to be dating a lawyer."

"Yeah, but it is God's plan for me to fall in love with her."

Why does he have to have the last word? This man, this man.

The boat ride in Lake Michigan and traveling around my beautiful city was everything.

Daryl is a very nice young man. I wonder if he is single. I have a couple of young ladies who would love to occupy his time. I should ask, but Noble will not like that because he hates it when I try to play matchmaker. I remember the time I tried to hook Natasha Janine up with Raq. That was a total disaster. I invited everyone to my place for dinner. I catered the food and had an interior designer come to my apartment and everything. It was perfect. The evening was designed for romance. We ate, played cards, drank all night, and danced the night away. Raq

told me he would take Natasha Janine home but instead, he took her to his place where he had another lady there. Natasha Janine said she was drunk but heard him call someone for a threesome. She swears she was totally against it, but when I mentioned it too Noble, he didn't seem surprised by the information which always makes me wonder if she really did take part in the threesome. She has not been the same since that night. The only thing Noble would say was I told you to stay out of it. When a man is not trying to hook his best friend up, something is definitely wrong with that dude and I should have known.

Noble says, "Baby do you want to stop for ice cream, a latte, tea, or anything before we head in?"

"No, I'm good. I wish you could carry me. I'm so tired."

"Babe, hop on my back it's not like we have far to walk."

"Ok, you have to kneel down so I can get on it."

I climb my grown ass on his back and sure enough, he carries me through the entrance to the elevator.

"You can put me down now."

He kneels down so I can get off.

"Thank you, baby. Did I hurt your back?"

"Not at all, to be quite honest it was so arousing, look at what you do to me."

I look down and see him, his pants bulging like his muscle needs to be free.

"Noble, were you like that when we entered the entrance and walked past all those people?"

"Yes!"

"You weren't embarrassed?"

"Hell no, I'm a grown ass man carrying a beautiful, sexy ass, educated woman on my back. If my muscle didn't get hard from an experience like that then it wouldn't be women I'm attracted to.

Did you see how happy the old man who was sitting in the chair was when we walked past him?"

"I did notice he was smiling."

"Babe, he acknowledged what was happening and was cheering me on."

"I can't believe you and I'm embarrassed."

"Well, you shouldn't be."

Then he walks up to me pressing me against the back of the elevator and picks me up so I can feel him. He is so bad, but I do love it.

We walk inside the condo.

"Noble, I need a shower to clean myself from the smell of people. We were on the Riverwalk, sitting on those benches and tossing around on the waves of Lake Michigan."

"Virgie, do you want me to join you?" He is always trying to find a way to be wet with me.

"No Noble, the point I'm making is I want to take a shower by myself."

"Okay, can I watch?"

"What Noble?" I'm wondering why he would want to do that like he hasn't seen my everything already.

"Can I watch you shower?"

Now he will sit and watch me wash my body that he has basically washed, "Suit yourself."

I go straight to the bathroom and turn the shower heads on so that the water will be good and hot. As I am taking off my clothes, this man comes into the bathroom with a chair. I'm saying to myself, "Really Noble!"

"Babe, pretend like I'm not here."

"How can I do that with you talking to me?"

"Okay babe, I will not say a word."

I continue to take my clothes off but for some odd reason, this has me all wet inside and aroused. You would have thought I was a stripper in the night club working for those dollars trying to make it rain. I am bending over, rubbing my legs, squatting, and taking my underwear off. I walk the walk. It seems like the longest walk ever to just get to the shower. I enter the glass doors and notice how excited his muscle was for this moment. When I say I'm performing in this shower, I am performing. I'm receiving all kinds of awards tonight. And I love every minute of it too! I took the sponge and was squeezing the water between these extensions rubbing the sponge against my sweet muscle.

Noble almost ran in this shower with his clothes on. I stopped him shaking my finger in his direction reminding him you are only here to watch which made him sit back down in that chair. I was squeezing these breasts and lathering them with soap. I saw a porno movie once where a lady tried to suck her own breast and I always wanted to try that, so I did. That thing right there had me wet and not just from the water. I'm talking about soaking wet. Noble watches me while touching his muscle and licking his lips but doesn't say a word. I bent over with my derrière facing him, cleaning myself really good. I want to make sure he sees everything. I think I have been in this shower for about 45 minutes. He is not saying a word, but oh is he absolutely enjoying this. He watches me like he is in the theatre watching a movie without blinking because if he did blink then the movie would be over. Let me get my tail out of this shower because I know I will not be resting anytime soon after this showcase. As I step out of the shower, Noble says, "Wow, I need a shower after that performance."

I laugh because the way he works me out on a regular I need a vacation.

Now we both are clean and freshly showered. I decide to lay down, but I have trained myself to go to sleep whenever I'm lying down.

"Virgie, are you asleep?"

"No, Noble I'm up!"

"I want to share something with you?"

"Okay let me sit up."

"Virgie, I hope you know it was the moment you touched me that I have never been the same. I had yearned for that touch of your soft caress against my arms like you did. I find myself daydreaming about everything we have done, places we have gone, and the things we have adventured upon. I'm working hard to perfect myself into a better version of me. You bring me so much joy and it is this joy I would not change for anyone in the world. I know that you have questions about the man I am, but I have worked so hard to move forward in my life that I am not

47

ready to share it all just yet. I will pour my soul out to you, but it has to be on my terms.

Today, I was not happy about the way I introduced Daryl to you. Virgie, you deserve so much better. I was caught up in the moment and excitement that I lost my head and reacted. Normally, I wouldn't allow my body to do the talking but I decided tonight we will rest but if you stay another night, I will not be able to promise that we rest tomorrow. It's probably because I'm going to try to make up for today."

We both laugh. Noble pulls me into his arms to cuddle and drifts off to sleep, but I'm wide awake. I appreciate him sharing; however, I still have questions and need answers, but I guess I will have to wait. I turn around to face him while I am lying in his arms. I love watching him sleep. He doesn't snore and he always sleeps so peacefully. I normally softly touch his face tracing the structure of his eyes, his lips, his beard, and his cheeks. I lean into him and kiss his lips by using my lips to trace them.

Noble doesn't move an inch, so I begin to share what my moments have been with him. I don't know why I feel so comfortable talking now while he sleeps but I do.

"Noble, this relationship has been everything I have ever imagined and prayed to encounter. I had started to believe that my opportunity for love had come and gone. The moment I hugged you I knew I needed you. I needed your love, the way you give it, your comfort, your understanding, your full attention, and the way you desire to have me. I knew from our first conversation about life that I would love you. Love you where you are. I know that there are so many other dimensions to you, and I want to take my time to discover them all. Your patient, kind, strong, loving, nurturing, giving, and the sexiest man I have ever met. Noble, I love you and you make me happy."

He opens his eyes, and it startles me making me jump.

"Virgie, thank you for your honesty."

"Noble, I thought you were asleep."

"I was asleep and then I felt your lips on mine, so I kept my eyes close to savor how sensual that felt. Then you started talking and I realized you were talking to me, so I listened to see if you were going to call another man's name out too." I hit him so fast in his arm, he plays way too much.

"You are so silly Mr. Noble."

"I'm serious babe."

"Why are you so open with me about your feelings when I'm asleep?

But you are black girl strong when I'm awake."

"I don't know Noble; I guess I gain my strongest confidence in the quietness of the room."

"Well baby, I will listen whenever you want to talk, but don't make me regret it and start talking so much that I need earplugs."

"I can't stand you, Mr. Noble."

"That's probably because I love keeping you on your back!" I hit him again. I can't be mad. I like that too.

We are still in bed and since we both are sharing. I say, "Noble, I need your help."

"Babe, what do you need? Anything? I am here for you."

"I often write notes to myself of how I would want to be pleased. Can I read a note that I wrote about you when I first met you?"

"By all means."

This will be my first time sharing my writing with him.

"I feel this is the best time to tell you since I have been green-lighted to share while you are awake," I say.

I then immediately grab my phone and go to my notes and start reading it.

"Here is my disclaimer, I have this wild imagination so don't judge me."

"Ms. Lady, can you just read it? I'm very curious about this note."

I read, "Can you help reach the peak of my explosion? I am so aroused that I am unable to stay still in my seat. I want to go to your house, and you lay me down on the table and have you peel off these stuffy clothes. I need you, man to take my shoes off first and then my socks. I wish you could caress these aching feet then wipe them clean before you suck on every one of these toes. I need you to pull my pants down so I may use my feet to stroke your man part as I watch it grow and grow and grow more. All the while, it becomes stronger and stronger. And, stronger. If only you could unfasten these pants with your teeth letting them grab my zipper to reveal the sight of my panties. Then you pull my panties down just low enough so you can rub your nose over the top of me. You should take your tongue and wet the top of her biting it slowly along the left then my right lip. Take these clothes off and spread me wide so you could see the full view of me. If you could stand not touching and watch how aroused my body is. I wish you would help me by taking your index finger and dipping it in me to press down toward my butt. Ooooh, you need to help me by taking it out and putting it in my mouth and watch me suck every drop of your finger. Then if you could take your mouth and kiss these lips one by one slightly biting at them as you move along my body. Help me!"

And before I could say the next word out of my mouth Noble was tongue kissing me while sucking the air right out of me.

"Baby, I can't take it anymore. Your words are putting me in a trance, and I can't hear anything else. The only thing I want to do is fulfill your written requests. I can feel everything we were doing in that note like it was only a note away. I want to do this narration piece so let's walk each other through this. I'm committing to pleasing you how you want and when you want. Virgie, what is it you need for me to do?"

I am laying here thinking, this is how we will begin making sure we both are getting what we need, and we are not going to stop any time soon. I will be staying here for a few more days or longer because he is not going to let me leave after hearing this note. And honestly speaking, I don't want to go.

Let me just say, Noble was focused on helping me. He helps me by entering his tongue in all of my openings and treating me like his last lollipop.

"Noble do you feel the release and use your mouth to take in what comes out?"

Yes indeed, he is helping me by positioning his hands under my cushion and thrusting his finger in my cushion opening pressing down towards the bed. Even though I didn't have to tell him, I did.

Sunday

"Noble baby please push it in and out. And out and in! Then flick your finger to thump the walls of my opening. Now, take it out and help me by placing it in your mouth."

And he did, just as I asked. This man is doing everything to me. I mean he is licking and sucking. Not to mention rubbing and thrusting all the while biting and nudging. He is even stroking and flipping and tossing salads and all. But he is still making sure I am comfortable, it's like he gets his best pleasure from me being comfortable. He is often pausing to whisper, "Are you okay? Does your leg hurt? Am I going too fast? Do you need to slow down? How does this feel?"

But before I could fully answer, we were right back at it. We had been at this all night long. I am having release after release. Then another release and after release. My body is going limp. We are both wiped completely out.

"Who are you Ms. Lady? We have never been so sensual on this level ever before. Why have you been holding your needs back? I am here to please you with all I have. To hear you read those words aloud to me, I wanted to suck your lips one by one. You write beautifully and you know exactly what you need. So again, I ask who you are?"

I close my eyes and say with all confidence, "I am Virgie."

"Virgie, where have you been my whole life?"

"That's the same question I have for you."

We lay in the silence of this moment. He then drifts back off to sleep.

But I'm still awake. I have cramps in my legs and abdomen. It feels like I have been lifting weights with my chest.

MONDAY

I reach to check my phone because when I'm with Noble I normally don't have any time to pay any attention to it or what's happening on social media. I love being with him! I don't want to leave! I still haven't shared this feeling either. I put my phone away when I am with him. I never get calls or texts when we are together. My time with him is uninterrupted. Wow, I have 56 text messages, 80 missed calls and not to mention hundreds of emails. Something has happened! Do I want to deal with this now? It's three o'clock in the morning. I better call my sisters, they called me a total of 64 times. I get out of bed which wakes Noble.

He says, "Baby what's wrong? Come back to bed, you need your rest."

"I will, I have some calls to make."

"Is everything okay?"

"I don't know." I wish I had some details for my own comfort, but I don't.

"You want me to get up with you?" He knows damn well he doesn't want to get out of bed.

"No, let me talk to my family and I will let you know what's going on when I get more information."

I call MJ and she answers on the first ring as if she knew I would be calling.

She says, "Virgie, where have you been?"

"I am at Noble's, what's the emergency? Twaab and Dominica have been blowing my phone up too."

"Sister, we thought something had happened to you."

"No, I'm good."

"Well, someone in your building was shot in a domestic disturbance and the management company will not release any information regarding this incident. I am so happy that you were with Mr. Noble reading your bible and praying together."

She is being real condescending because she knows what two grown single people are doing, but I will play along. Even though, I almost screamed with laughter because if she knew all of the sexual things we were doing, baby bye! Anyway, who am I fooling? She definitely knows she is a grown ass woman.

"Virgie, I think you should either stay over there or come stay with me.

I hate that you live in that area. I don't want you to go back there."

"MJ, it's my home." She hates that I live in the hood.

"MJ, let me call Twaab because she was with Natasha Janine yesterday and maybe she has more information."

"Love you Virgie Mae and tell Mr. Noble that he is always welcome to come and share what he knows at bible study."

"Whatever MJ! You really don't want to know. You don't even have an idea of what you are asking for because his skills aren't no joke. He can singlehandedly change the relationship world. Sister, trust me when I say this, he is great."

"Bye Virgie Mae, I will call your name out when I pray."

"Oh okay, thanks sister and pray for my Noble too," and I end the call.

I call Twaab but she doesn't answer so I have no other choice but to call Dominica. Now, she is letting this phone ring and ring.

Finally, she answers. "Dominica, did you call me?"

"Yeah, sister because someone got shot, killed, and stabbed at your place."

Let me just say there is only an ounce of truth in any story she is telling so I know I will have to spend my whole-time deciphering what is true or not. So, I just keep listening to her talk. She says, "Yeah they said your boyfriend's girlfriend came over there and yawl started arguing. She supposedly left, then came back with some dudes and started shooting. I went over there, but they had that place locked down saying something about an off-duty police officer got shot. You good though?"

"Yes Dominica, I am fine."

"Well, I told Twaab that as soon as the police cleared it out. I'm going to get that bitch. Who is she, sister?"

I wanted to play along but her mind is not right, and it would make matters even worse, so I told her the truth. I can't believe she still is asking, "So you are dating an off-duty police officer?" This is the whole reason why I didn't want to call her. She will create this whole new story line and it is usually funny and then I just start laughing. I really can't help but to laugh because this lady is too funny. After all of the explaining I did, she didn't hear a word I said. This lady cracks me up.

"Dominica, He is not a police officer."

"Then what does he do for a living?"

I had to take a second and think about it. I don't know what Noble does for a living. Whenever we start to discuss his career, he changes the topic. We are spending so much time enjoying each other's company I haven't even pressed the issue. The only information about his career I have is that he took a leave of absence and he has money put away.

"He is unemployed, Dominica!"

"With all your smarts you done let some clown ass man trick you out of your money."

"Girl, hell no!"

"I'm not judging you Virgie, but they have said it time and time again, it's the smart ones that are so stupid. I can't believe you fell for some unemployed man, who is not trying to get no job, living downtown in a foreclosure."

"What the hell are you talking about Dominica? Does your man have a job?"

"No, he doesn't Virgie, but I don't have a job either so like MJ always says you must be equally yoked. You are the damn fool who is not yoked. You're working and he is home playing house." She starts laughing too hard. I can't stand her!

"Bye I'm going to bed little sister."

"Yeah, Virgie because with that lien on his property this may be the last night yawl can sleep in that bed," and hangs up.

I could hear her laughing as the call ended.

My sister Dominica is right. What if he is selling me on all this sex to steal my money? Is this place really his or is he house sitting? There are no pictures of real people around here. The door man never calls him by his name. I knew something was too good to be true. I should have my police friend run his information. Natasha Janine told me a long time ago to do that, but I got my ass caught up in this sex, sexual escapades, play on words foolishness with him. He is probably sitting around all day thinking of shit to say to sound all seductive. I knew it was strange that I just couldn't say words like fuck, cum, penis and pussy. Working men do not have time to think of words for a woman's anatomy. Noble would say the sounds of those words have no passion behind them. Who the hell is this man? And he got the nerve to ask me who I am? I should wake his ass up and get to the bottom of this. My phone vibrates and it's Twaab.

"Hey Virg, I just talked to Dominica, you got her dying laughing. It was hard but I made out some of the stuff she was saying you all talked about."

"What did she say?"

"She said that Noble was an off-duty police officer that got fired for shooting his ex-girlfriend. The ex-girlfriend told you that Noble stole her house and sent it in foreclosure and yawl hiding out there until the bank took it."

I burst out laughing so loudly that it woke Noble up.

"Babe, is everything ok?"

"Yes, I'm laughing at Twaab."

He says, "Okay," and goes back to sleep.

"Twaab, let me get off this phone and I will call you in the morning."

I hang up. As I am walking back in the room, I wonder how I let Dominica put the charging cable on me. But one thing is for sure, I need more information and I need it like yesterday about Mr. Noble.

"Morning', sleepyhead." I say as I am actually rubbing his head.

"Good morning my Virgie!"

"Did you sleep well last night Mr. Noble?"

"Yes, I did! How did you sleep babe?"

"Noble, I didn't sleep well. I have been up all night wondering why I know so little about you."

"Virgie, are you hungry?"

"This is what I am talking about."

"What are you talking about babe?"

"Whenever I ask questions about you, you change the subject. You know everything about me."

55

"Virgie, you are a person who loves to talk and sometimes it is solely about yourself."

"Oh really?"

"Okay, Ms. Virgie? Let me adjust my eyes. I'm ready to know what you want to know but I'm not an open book because there are things I'm still dealing with and I'm not at a place in my life to discuss yet. And I really mean yet. I need for you to be patient with me and in due time all will be explained."

Now, Dominica may be right about him. He is some broke ass clown trying to trick me out of my money.

"Noble, do you have a girlfriend?"

"I'm too old to have a girlfriend. You are the only woman in my life other than my mother and sister."

He has never even mentioned his mother or sister before.

"Where is your mother?"

"She lives in Florida with her brother, and she suffers from dementia."

"I'm sorry to hear that. How long has she had it?"

"It's been a while. She lives with him because he is retired and could provide her with the care she needs. But I thought the questions were about me."

"They are about you. How long have you been single?"

"Almost three years before meeting you."

"Is this really your place without any liens on it?"

"Yes, it is and please explain Ms. Lady why I would have liens on my property."

"Don't try to distract me. I'm asking the questions."

"I can tell now; you didn't get any sleep because you are quite the grumpy lady when you're sleepless in Chicago."

"Whatever! What do you do for a living Mr. Noble?"

"I am a doctor." He plays way too much. I know I didn't hear him correctly.

"You are a what?" I bet he won't say it again. He doesn't know when to stop playing.

"Doctor!" Doctor really! He is lying! He is not a doctor! Doctor, and came up with this on his own.

"Be serious." I need him to tell the truth and stop playing.

"I'm a doctor. I have been practicing internal medicine for fourteen years." A real doctor, is this man serious? He says he is! A doctor I don't believe him.

"Noble, if you are a doctor how do you take a leave of absence from that?" Doctors are like marines; they are always on the job.

"I needed a break, so I took time off."

"This is where I need a break from the questions because now the questions are needing details, and this is where I struggle with answering the details of my life. I have been on a leave of absence for almost three years. Now, let's start over."

Something traumatic had to happen because he refused to discuss this situation.

"Good morning Virgie," and he leans in to kiss me and I can't help it, but I'm kissing him back. His lips are always so soft. I can't believe I have been dating a doctor the whole time. This explains how he knows how to hit every spot in my body oh so right. Noble has been operating on me and I love it. Natasha Janine is going to hit the roof once I tell her this. We both thought he was some kind of trust fund baby, but a doctor! We would have never guessed that one.

"Noble, my whole family was calling me yesterday, so I called them last night. They said a couple of days ago there was some type of domestic disturbance that occurred in my building. MJ said that it involved some shooting incident. If it's okay with you, can I stay over here?"

"Virgie, you don't have to ask me that."

He gets up from the bed and goes to a drawer in his nightstand and hands me a Gucci key ring with a set of keys on it.

I say, "Did you send the shooters to my building because you have keys ready after I tell you what happened?"

"No ma'am, I didn't but if that's what it took then I should have thought of it a long time ago. You are free to come and go anytime you want. My home is your home and I know you will not be as open to your home as I am."

"Why would you say that?"

"Virgie, you are a protector of your space. That's why you shy away from close encounters with me. Our souls are tied and there is no way I'm letting go of that. I didn't sleep well because you didn't sleep. I heard you on the phone and could sense you were worked up about something. I have learned since being with you I have to allow you to release when you feel ready. I mean release in every aspect of your life. This is why touching those sensual spots on your body is slow and methodical. I need for you to reach a level of relaxation where your body allows me to be the instrument you use for your control. So, when you shared what you had written the night we met, I lost control. I was taken by surprise. This muscle was pulsating so hard. I thought I was going to burst a blood vessel. From the time our bodies connected I knew I would love you." He looks over and notices that I am crying.

"Baby, you good?"

Then he reaches over and holds me tightly kissing my forehead.

I whispered, "I am so nervous about this feeling I have for you.

Everyone keeps telling me that this won't last, and everything is not what it seems, so I guard my "release" as you say because I'm afraid. I have never experienced sexual pleasure like this, love like this, the attention from my man like this, protection nor this desire to never leave your side. Noble, I knew the moment I felt your heartbeat that I would want to listen to its rhythm forever. I'm scared of this feeling."

"Baby, I'm just as scared. I loved hard once and now I must love again. I vowed to never try again, and you walked frantically up to me and changed my mind."

Now, I'm crying with snot bubbles on his chest. He doesn't say another word and just lets me get everything all out.

"Virgie, are you going into the office today?"

"Yes! Because staying here, would have us in bed all day long."

"Now babe, you know that's not a bad idea."

"See, that's why I'm definitely going to work."

"Well, if you insist. Can I touch you in the shower?"

"Well, if you insist, Mr. Noble."

"I do!"

"Then, Yes you may."

Noble gets up and walks to the shower and I could hear the water being turned on. I lay in the bed waiting and thinking he is going to return to the room, but he didn't. When I walk in the bathroom, he is standing at the sink brushing his teeth.

"Mr. Noble, what are you doing?"

"I'm making sure my breath is fresh because the only taste I desire to have in my mouth is the taste of you."

I smirk and say, "I guess I better brush mine too."

His muscle popped out so hard that it hit the sink and I tried not to laugh but I couldn't help it. We both started laughing after he said ouch. You see, I had never put my mouth on his muscle before. He had never asked and well I never volunteered. So, I understand why it is so exciting, it will finally feel the fullness of these lips wrapped around it. It will feel the warmth of my tongue, the smoothness of the inside of my mouth and the squeeze of these lips. I look over at him in the mirror and he has turn bloodshot red in the face. This is going to be fun. I will be in control of his release and let's see how he likes it.

I haven't experienced a shower like this. It is all steamy like a sauna. Noble changes the setting on the dials because the water is coming out all misty. I feel like we were in an X-rated movie scene and I don't care who happens to be watching. He enters the shower first and walks straight into the water as if it is calling his name. I waited before I entered because I felt like he needed a minute to be alone in there. As I enter, I walk right into his butt and caress his back. With every single touch to his body, I can actually feel his body's response. He grasps for air like he has never been touched before.

"Noble can I please you this time?" I'm asking but I'm going to do it anyway even if he says, "No!"

"Babe, no, let me please you." Why does he have to do all the pleasing? I want a turn.

"But I want to please you, let me help you to release." Yeah, let me please you, he is always in charge. Well, he is the man in this relationship. But I don't care if he is, I want to do this.

"Virgie, you want me to let you please me but all I want is to please you. When you feel good then that's what pleases me."

59

"Well, right now at this moment my desire is to please you Noble and that will make me feel better."

So, before he could reply, I just went for it. Noble is so good to me and since we have been together, he has made it his top priority to please me. He has made every muscle in my body sing with delight and if I could repay him back some of what he has done for me I will be ecstatic. I immediately took control. I rub his back softly allowing for him to feel every touch of my fingertips. His body began collapsing within my arms. I took my hands and started rubbing his chest, grabbing and pulling at his skin. I kissed his back, his shoulders, pressed my pillows up against the small of his back. He turns around towards me and I drop to my knees. Noble stood there strong and powerful, but when I took his muscle in my mouth everything changed. He is pleased. He is calling my name, rubbing my head while moaning and groaning.

Even though I don't pride myself on being all that, let me just say, I impressed myself. I went to town. I don't know if it is because of the steam from the shower but my mouth is filled with fluids. I am working my tongue around the front of it, sucking at his sacs, and then making sure he hits the back of my mouth. I heard him moaning with ecstasy. He is enjoying it because he is gripping the hell out of my head. I need to brace myself for the release. I'm a big girl! I can do this. I have never swallowed anything, but I feel like this is what I should be doing. But what if it tastes disgusting? What am I talking about? He has put his mouth all over me and I can't do this one thing. Okay I will do it and I'm going to do it without even thinking about it. Here I go. I look up at him and he is rubbing all of his chocolate-colored skin and with the steam and misty water hitting his body he appears to be glowing. I smile. I feel delighted knowing it's me who is making him so aroused and then I hear him calling my name.

"Virgie, oh Virgie, baby you are taking me places, this feels so good, baby oh baby, I'm there I'm on the edge of releasing, baby stop baby baby, baby."

And before I could even move it happened and I closed my eyes and swallowed. Oh my, when I tell Natasha Janine this, she is going to go crazy. Noble lifts me up off the floor and hugs me tightly.

"Virgie, that's the first time you have done that isn't it?"

"No, I do this all the time," and we both bust out laughing.

"Thank you baby I needed that. I love you so much."

"You are welcome and thank you for allowing me to please you."

He grabs my face and kisses me with so much passion that it makes me think about taking the day off.

"Babe, you're going to work so don't think about staying home and getting all of this loving." I laugh again, he always seems to know what I'm thinking.

"You were thinking that it is written on your forehead."

"No, it's not!"

He makes me sick thinking he knows everything.

"Virgie, I would like to stay locked up in this house with you but truthfully speaking, I have errands I need to run today that must be completed."

It felt like we were dressed and on our way down Michigan Avenue towards my office building. Today is a beautiful day. The advantage of staying at Noble's condo is that it is down the street from my office. As we are pulling up, I see Natasha Janine walking towards the building. Natasha Janine is also an attorney in the building too, but we work in different offices. I'm a business contract attorney and Natasha Janine is a defense attorney. Before I knew it, she spotted us pulling up to the main entrance. Noble says, "There's your girl!" I see her and wave at my friend. I have this "girl I can't wait to tell you what happened this weekend smile" on my face and Natasha Janine recognizes it immediately and starts smiling so hard too.

Noble says, "Guess she's excited about seeing you or excited about getting the details of our weekend."

"I don't tell her about our moments."

"Virgie, you know that's not true. I can tell by the way she treats me. I get it, you need an outlet, and she is that for you. Have a great day baby!

If you need me to pick you up, let me know."

"Mr. Noble, I will be home later because I have keys, I can let myself in."

"Oh okay, well I'll make sure the house is clean and dinner is ready for you Ms. Lady," then kisses me before he gets out to open my door.

Natasha Janine says, "Hey Noble! How are you?"

"Natasha Janine, I'm great thanks for asking. How are you doing?"

She says, "I can't complain and with these clients of mine, they don't listen anyway."

We all start laughing. Natasha Janine is funny.

"Ladies have a great day, and baby I will see you later until then I am thinking of you."

"See you later sweetie," says Natasha Janine while she is standing up here smiling and all.

I hit her on her arm so hard. "Ouch, I am just joking," she replies.

I give her the "girl stop playing so damn much look" you know the one where you are frowned up rolling your eyes. She is funny but not that funny.

"Girl cut it out. He already thinks I share our moments with you."

"You do?"

"Yeah, I do, but if you're going to keep giving it away then I will need to stop. He doesn't want you to know all the things he does to this body," moving my hand down the side of my skirt.

"Well, you shouldn't tell me if he doesn't want me to know."

"You are right about that so I will stop."

"Damn! Really? You're tripping!"

"You just told me to stop telling you and now I'm tripping for saying I will."

"No, you are tripping for even having this discussion with me. We share everything and I may have smiled a little too hard a couple times, but you know I wouldn't step out of line with the information."

"I was just about to tell you that I swallowed this morning. Yep, I did that!"

"What the fuck are you talking about? You swallowed, I'm so proud of you! We have to celebrate. What are you doing for lunch today?"

"I need to go over some contracts, but I should be good?"

"Come here and give me a hug, I'm so proud of my baby."

"Girl, shut the hell up." We both started laughing and then proceeded through the doors, lobby and then got on the elevator.

"Virgie, call me later. I should be in the office all day because I'm prepping for a trial."

"Ok, I sure will."

I feel buzzing in my purse. I grab my cell phone and it's my Auntie. "Hey Auntie!"

Natasha Janine is standing next to me, all up in my business and says, "Tell her hi."

"Auntie, Natasha Janine says hi." My Auntie probably can hear her in the background anyway.

"Virgie Mae, tell her I said, "Hi bitch!" Auntie thinks Natasha Janine is a user and she doesn't like that about her. I tell her all the time we use each other that's what friends are for. She disagrees.

Natasha Janine and I both bust out laughing. My auntie has no buffer; she says whatever comes to her mind. Natasha Janine gets off the elevator still laughing and says, "Bye bitch!"

"Bye girl." She knows how crazy my Auntie is and she take whatever she gives out.

"Auntie, what's up? My cell phone may lose connection because I'm still on the elevator, but I will call you back."

"Okay, I will call you when I get to the office. Love you."

If she is calling this early in the morning something is wrong. This lady doesn't even get up before 10 am and definitely doesn't start talking on the phone until after lunch. I walk into the office and pass the reception desk taking big strides. I have finally had my grown woman moment, when I took my man's penis in my mouth. I'm feeling myself right now because I have on my big girl drawers and they can't tell me anything. As I step into my office, my phone is ringing. I answer it on speaker because I haven't even put my things down yet.

"Hello, this is Virgie Mae Kelly. How may I help you?"

"Hey Virg, this is your man Kelle." I'm saying to myself Kelle is definitely a damn fool. He hasn't been my man in almost two years.

"Hello Kelle, how may I help you?" He is probably calling because he paid for our breakfast and now, he thinks I owe him.

"I had been calling you all weekend, so I decided to catch you at the office." I did see I had missed his call, but I purposefully ignored his calls. He knows this.

"Okay, what is it you need?" I'm sure, nothing. He doesn't want a thing, calling to bug me.

"I was making some deliveries this weekend and I guess I delivered some food to your man's house." I say to myself, "My man's house," wow. He is nosey as hell.

"What do you mean my man's house?" What does he really want?

"Well, this young man came to the door to retrieve the delivery. I had met him before when he and his friend came to the restaurant a while back." Was that Kelle at the door? Damn, it probably was his ass.

"But how do you know it's my man?"

"I recognized your purse by the door because it is the Louis Vuitton hobo bag that I bought you and had engraved with the letters VMK."

"Kelle, you are calling me to say what?"

"Well, I want to tell you that he doesn't deserve you and that the friend I saw him at the restaurant with was a woman."

"Well, it isn't a crime to have a woman as a friend," I say irritated with him and his need to share.

"Well, I am just trying to warn you to guard your heart. I know how hard you love, and I don't want you to end up hurt."

"Thank you for calling to warn me, take care." His ass is not trying to warn me. He is fucking with my happiness because he isn't happy.

"Virg, wait a minute when do you want to set up the play date with Nuri?"

"Kelle, let me check my schedule and get back to you." In other words, not a chance in hell.

"Okay let us know." I will definitely not! I'm not going anywhere with yawl asses, fuck off and never call again.

I ended the call and immediately became sick to my stomach. What the fuck just happened here? So, Noble took a bitch to Kelle's and Kelle's has to be the one to tell me. Wake me up from this nightmare. This man is lying, lying to me about his relationship. Noble is a liar! Why is he lying to me and treating me like some low-class ass woman? He couldn't be honest. This man has a whole other relationship. I "swallowed!" Damn, I'm mad as hell. I can't work after getting this kind of news. What the fuck has just happened? And Kelle has to be the one to tell me. This is the craziest shit I have ever heard. Kelle, with his nosey ass. I saw that Louis Vuitton hobo bag I bought you sitting by the door. Now, my phone is ringing again and it's Mr. Noble himself.

"Hello!"

"Hey babe, checking to see if you're ok."

"What do you mean by that?"

"As I pulled away, I saw you and your friend were out there hitting each other. Everything ok?"

"No everything is not okay," I snapped.

"What happened? I thought you two all were good."

"We are good, but everything is not ok with us."

"What do you mean?"

"You have a girlfriend?"

"You are my girlfriend! I can't believe I am even saying that I'm too old to be discussing if you are my girlfriend," he laughs at my question."

"He he hell, this shit isn't funny!"

"What are you talking about? What's wrong with you?"

"You had the nerve to take a bitch to the restaurant that my ex owns and wouldn't think it would get back to me."

"Virgie, what are you talking about?"

"I just received a call informing me of you being a player and how I need to guard my heart."

"Babe, this isn't a conversation I want to have with you over the phone."

"Why? Is she with you and you can't talk?"

"Virgie, I need you to calm down and think about what you are saying. Does any of it make sense? I have a girlfriend and I took her to a restaurant your ex-boyfriend owns?"

"Noble, I don't know what the fuck to believe and I have so much work do today I don't even have time to deal with this shit."

"Babe, I would like to talk about this. When can you let me know what time you are available to talk? Or can we talk when you get here later? I hope whoever felt the need to share this bullshit with you knows how upset this shit has made you."

"I'll talk to you later."

"Babe, I love you and I don't have the time or patience for anything other than love. Bye babe."

So, he is so upset that he is cursing at me. I need to talk to Natasha Janine. I need to call her. Her phone barely even rings and she is answering it, I don't even let her say hello I start talking immediately.

"Natasha Janine, can you talk?"

"Yeah, I have been thinking about you. What is going on?"

"Girl, Noble ass has a girlfriend!"

"What? Get the fuck out of here."

"Yes, girl! He has a girlfriend!"

"Did the bitch call you or something? How do you know?"

"Girl, Kelle's ass just called to tell me. He saw me over Noble's house this weekend and wanted to let me know."

"Kelle saw what? How the hell did he know you were at Noble's and then saw you there? I can't stand his nosey ass."

"Girl, he told me that Noble brought his girlfriend to the restaurant and he remembered him when he came over with the food and saw my bag sitting by the door that he bought me."

"What bag did he buy you with his cheap ass?"

"That Louis Vuitton hobo bag with my initials on it."

"Girl, shut the damn door."

"That's what he said."

"So, you're telling me that Kelle saw the Louie bag that you let me use when I went out of town. Now, you know I haven't even returned the bag to you yet."

"What are you talking about Natasha Janine?"

"You heard what I said. I still have that bag. Remember you just asked me about that bag last week?"

"Are you serious? I just went the hell off on Noble. Why did Kelle's stupid ass have to lie?"

"Because you keep thinking that clown ass man has your best interest at heart."

"Then how does he know that I was with Noble?"

"He might have a microchip in your ass. You stayed drunk when you were fucking around with him, who knows."

"Girl, I'm about to fuck around and lose a good man because I am still fucking around with Kelle and his shit."

"You can say that again. Kelle is fucking with your head because he knows you believe everything, he tells you. His ass is mad you found someone, and it is not him."

"Girl, my Aunt is calling me, and I haven't called her back yet. Give me a raincheck on lunch. I have to make this right with Noble."

"Go get your man, we can always talk. Love you!"

"Love you too, and thanks for helping me with this."

"Anytime!"

How stupid could I be I should have called her first before I said something to Noble. "Damn!"

I call my Auntie back. "Hey Auntie, what's up?"

"Hey baby, I want to apologize first."

"Apologize for what?"

"Child, you know Mr. Sid has been working my ass out and the other day I was running my damn mouth like I always do."

"Okay?"

"Child, he was telling me how depressed Kelle has been since yawl broke up, so I told him, the hell with Kelle slow ass that you got you a new man from what MJ told me. His dumb ass start asking me all kind of questions and my ass just kept talking."

"Auntie, it's cool."

"No, it is not because Kelle's weak ass needs to move on with his life and I did my best to help him with that. Forgive your old ass auntie.

That liquor was making me do some strange things," and then she started laughing too hard.

"Auntie, did you tell him I was with Noble this weekend."

"No, but Sid's crazy ass did hear MJ tell me that when we were discussing all that shit happening in your building."

"Don't worry about it, I understand completely."

"But please know I did check Sid's ass because he was in my kitchen talking on the phone repeating shit. Afterwards I explained how fucked up this shit is. He's sorry too and he said next time you come to the restaurant he will make it up to you."

"Tell Mr. Sid, I'm not mad and it will be a long time before I return. I see my patronage there is not helping Kelle to move on with his life.

So, I need to help him before I hurt him for real this time."

"Child, I understand. He so damn dumb that he can't understand why a woman would not want a weak ass man who can't keep his shit together. I'm sorry again and let's make some time to go shopping, you know I do not have a dime to my name. Bye baby!"

"Bye Auntie!

Now, I don't know who I should be madder at, Kelle or my damn self. Why would I listen to that damn man? Why? Because he keeps telling me he cares about me. I should be mad at my damn self. He doesn't care about me because if he did, we would still be together. Me and my damn separation and loss issues. I got to hold down every sorry ass relationship I have ever had. Kelle with his jealous hating ass. I need some counseling because I got some real issues. This is a big fuck up, and after all I am still doing for Kelle's ass. The next time he calls me for some legal advice I'm sending his ass a bill. It's apparent why he is single, and it didn't work out with Cheryl big ass. He was painting the picture to me that it was her, but I see he played a role in it too. Kelle acted like she did him so wrong, yeah, I bet. His stupid ass probably did her wrong. I remember she called me to say she wanted to talk. I told her flat out I will not have a discussion with my man's ex-wife. She was probably trying to tell me something I should know. This is really fucked up. How am I going to tell Noble that Kelle called me and lied? This is really fucked up. I better get started working because Noble will be calling back any minute.

Monday

Time flew by. I look up at my desk clock and notice the time. It has just dawned on me that Noble hasn't even called, wait a minute, Noble hasn't called me at all. Let me check to see if he left a voice message, text or email. He could have called, and I was so consumed with work I didn't hear my desk phone, or my cell phone vibrate. "Virgie, who the fuck are you kidding," he didn't call. I tell myself. I have been buried in contracts at my desk that I haven't even eaten anything. I'm going to check anyway. Hell no! Not one single message was left from Noble.

I have fucked up! I have fucked up big time! I'm calling him now. I dialed the numbers so fast I don't even remember what I pressed. It's just ringing and ringing. Damn, I have really fucked up for real I'm not playing. Let me hang up this phone, I need to leave this office. I have fucked this up royally. I'm going over there now. Let me call me an Uber. Do I even have the keys? Let me look for them. Hell no! Damn, damn, and damn! I have fucked this thing up fucking around with

Kelle's sad ass. What was I thinking? If he had called Noble with this shit, it would have bothered him too. My cell phone vibrates. It's Noble. Thank God!

"Hello Mr. Noble." I need to check his temperature.

"Hey Virgie! What's up? I was taking a nap." What is this "Hey Virgie," shit? Damn! He isn't calling me babe. Damn!

"You hadn't called me, so I got worried."

"Worried about what?"

He acts like nothing happened; this shit is bad.

I say softly and seductively to see if his temperature will change, "You hadn't called."

"I thought you needed some time to process all of the stuff you were saying earlier, and that you would call me."

"No, I'm good I don't need to process. I'm going to take an Uber over there."

"Oh okay, I'm here."

"Did I leave the keys there?"

"Yes, you did, the keys are on the nightstand."

"Okay well, I'm on my way. I will see you in a few." "Oh, see you soon," and he hangs up.

I really have fucked up! Oo wee, I'm so fucked right now. He won't even come and pick me up. This right here is bad. Oo wee! This is bad, really bad!

I have been in this Uber forever and this man won't stop talking. It normally takes a couple of minutes to Noble's place and it feels like we have been riding in this car for an hour. Noble is mad, and mad as hell. What does that really look like? I have never seen him mad, upset or even bothered. I need to brace myself. What if he yells? Is he aggressive when he is trying to make a point? He may be the type of person who nags. I don't know anything about this man, and I have repeated some dumb shit that I never verified but acted as if it was true. I have made a law student mistake thinking everything stated is fact. I should have gone home. Too late now. We have stopped right in front of the building. The Uber driver is looking at me because I am just sitting in this car like this isn't my destination. I'm just sitting here.

"Ma'am, we have reached your destination."

"Thank you so much sir," I replied hesitantly.

I get out of the car and walk to the door.

The doorman Anthony says, "Hello Ms. Kelly. Mr. Winston has informed us that you would be arriving soon. Do you need help with anything?"

"No Anthony, I am good. I only have my laptop and purse."

How stupid am I? I look down and actually realized I'm so stupid because I really am. I'm listening to Kelle's ass and didn't even realize that I'm carrying my turquoise Celine' bag and it's the bag I have had with me this past weekend. If I would have just looked, listened, and thoroughly heard what I heard, I would be upstairs right now being pleased by my man. But no, I have my ass down here walking the long walk to the door with this stupid ass look on my face. I have really fucked this up real fast. I get on the elevator with this fine guy. He is light skin with a low cut and a tailored suit.

This man says, "Hello Ma'am!"

"Hello!" He is fine and smelling great too.

"What floor would you like?" He asks.

"Can you press thirteen for me?"

"Sure, that's where I'm going also."

"Okay, thank you."

The elevator door opens and we both are walking down the hall. Where is he going? The only condo down this way is Noble's. I ask myself who is this man. Why is he going to Noble's house?

So, I ask, fuck it! If he doesn't want to say then he just doesn't say, "Excuse me, are you going to 1315?"

"Why yes? Is that where you are going also Ma'am?"

"Yes, I'm going to see Mr. Winston."

"Mr. Winston," I don't think I ever heard anyone refer to him as Mr. Winston."

And, before either of us could knock on the door Noble opened it and says, "What's up, Jon?"

I know he is not greeting this man before he greets me. He is definitely mad!

"Hey babe, let me take your bags," then kisses me on my left cheek.

"Virgie, have you met Jon?"

"Well, we haven't actually met. Hello Jon, I'm Virgie."

Noble reiterates what I say and says, "Jon this is Virgie."

Jon says, "I finally get to meet the infamous Virgie who stole my friend's heart."

I smile but what the hell is he talking about? There is nothing infamous about me, everything I do is grand.

Noble interrupts my thought and says, "Virgie, this is Dr. Jon Tapes."

Jon walks to the kitchen, opens the refrigerator and asks, "What do you have to eat? I'm hungry."

"Jon, I thought you want to talk."

Jon replies, "I do."

Then Noble says, "Well let's go out and we can grab something while we are out."

I walk to the bedroom to settle down. Noble stayed in the living room with Dr. Tapes. Shortly after, Noble comes into the bedroom and says, "I'm about to step out with Jon. I know we need to talk, but he needs my help, and we can talk when I get back."

"Okay!" I know we must talk, I fucked up and I have to take ownership of this shit.

I walked up to Noble to give him a kiss and he turned his head so I could kiss his cheek.

"I'm sorry Noble, if that means anything."

"Babe it means everything, but we'll talk when I get back."

Noble starts walking to the door then turns and says, "You know I love you!"

But he didn't wait for a response and that didn't keep me from answering, "I know, and I love you too."

I can't rest. Noble calls and asks, "What are you doing?"

"Nothing looking over some files. You miss me."

"Babe always! Do you want me to bring you something home to eat?"

"Sure, I'm hungry and too lazy to get up and fix something."

"Well, we are wrapping up and I should be home soon."

"Okay. Will you still think about me until you see me?"

"Virgie my feelings for you haven't changed. Something is going on with you and we need to talk about that."

"I know, I'm sorry for it all, but we'll talk when you get in."

After the call ends, I feel like crap. Why do I allow people to influence the decisions I have made about my love life? I don't owe anyone anything. I need to just stop it. I'm going to call Natasha Janine. I type in her number and she answers immediately.

"Hey girl? What are you doing?"

"Who is that I hear in the background?" Why is my sister over there again?

"Well, okay then I will see you tomorrow and tell Twaab to call me later since I have to call you to talk to her. Bye girl!"

Now I'm sitting in the house bored to death. Maybe I should watch a movie until Noble comes home since there is nothing else to do.

TUESDAY

I'm awakened by Noble's kiss.

"Virgie, you tired baby?"

"I guess, I thought I was watching a movie, but the movie must have been watching me. What time is it?"

"Babe, it's after midnight."

"What? I thought you would be home soon." Wow, it's really that late.

I must have slept for a while, for it to be this late.

"I came straight home after hearing you on the phone and decided I would get with Jon tomorrow."

"Noble, so how long have you been here?"

"About two hours."

"So, what were you doing for all of that time?"

"I was watching you sleep; I love to watch you sleep. I often do that whenever we sleep together. You make this cute snoring sound." "I don't snore Mr. Noble!' I say while rolling my eyes playfully. "Oh okay, I guess you can hear yourself in your sleep Ms. Lady." His playful sense of humor is back because he knows I don't snore. Well, I don't think I do.

"Why didn't you wake me so we could talk?"

"Because I decided to watch you sleep first. I saw that you weren't sleeping peacefully, so I woke you up. I don't want to talk about what happened right at this moment. I know we do need to talk but not at this time of morning."

"Noble, I want to say…"

"Virgie, not now. It's been a long day and I don't want to spend this night like we spent yesterday."

"Okay I understand. Let me get up and take these clothes off and get into my gown."

"No, just let me hold you." I feel awful, I have really fucked this up! "Okay." He doesn't even know how much I need this; I love him.

He extends his arms out and wraps them around me. We are lying in the silence of his room. Not a word being said between us.

73

"Virgie, how many times were you hurt by a man you loved?" The question takes me by surprise.

He repeats the question, "Tell me how many times you've been hurt?"

"Noble, I am ashamed to admit it, but I have been hurt so many times that I stopped counting."

"Now tell me Virgie, how many times were you loved in your relationships, I mean deeply loved, loved wholeheartedly?"

"Only once." Should I tell him, he is the only person who has made me feel this way?

"Babe, I'm here to love you like you have never been loved, but you have to let go of this stuff."

"What stuff is that?"

"The stuff that tells you, you are not worthy." I couldn't say a word and to be honest I didn't think any words needed to be said.

We are laying in the bed fully dressed which I know is strange for Noble, but he isn't complaining or saying anything. He is so quiet.

"Noble, are you asleep?"

"No babe, what's wrong?"

"Noble, have you ever been hurt?"

"Yes! Of course, I have been hurt before."

"How did you get over it?"

"Babe, I made the decision to love again."

"So, you have only been hurt once?"

"Yes, and it wasn't any fault of mine. Love has walked back into my life and I want it to stay here because it feels good to love again. I love how it makes me feel to love, care, and provide for the woman in my life. I'm very protective of the time we share together. I had plans to talk to Jon over here, but because we were experiencing "something" I asked him to take me to a bar instead. I knew when you walked through that I wouldn't be able to give him my attention when you came home because my attention belongs to you."

"Thank you, Noble."

"You're thanking me for what?"

"For being you, I love that about you Noble." And here I go, crying softly well I thought I was.

Tuesday

"Baby, why are you crying?"

"I don't know. I felt terrible all day because I told myself, you fucked this up and the way you were acting made me think it was true."

"Babe, I'm here, and I'm not going anywhere but if you need to cry so that you can let go the stuff that's bottled up inside of you then cry. I will ask you if I can wipe your eyes with my shirt or with some tissue," while he is smiling at me. "I'm yours baby as fucked up as I am, I'm all yours!"

"I wouldn't have you any other way Mr. Noble."

I am so aroused but Noble is sleeping. I wanted to take advantage of our "moment" making up for the shit I did. Our "moment" has now come upon us, I start moving swiftly so he will not be able to stop me. I rolled over and took the covers off of Noble and started rubbing his muscle over his pants. I take my hands and place it under his shirt and rub my hand over his nipples. I raise up his shirt so I can kiss his chiseled chest. I put my hand in his sweatpants to pull out his muscle and watched it grow and grow and grow. The smooth black skin expands in length and width. It was at this "moment" he opened his eyes. He says, "take it easy this isn't a race." He takes his shirt off over his head displaying his muscular chest. I lay witnessing the stiffness of his muscle extend to the center of his chest as he lays back as I continue my battery. It's so long, hard and yet soft all at the same time. He leans in to kiss my lips. I know the sight of me biting on them is driving him wild. The "moment" I felt his lips against mine was my opportunity to return to how we were the day before. This return back in time that will never be erased. The "moment" he reaches for my hand is his way to speak nonverbally to me. It is this "moment" I grab hold of his face and begin to delight in the smoothness of his skin. The "moment" he whispers to me while I'm on top of him kissing his neck, "touch my chest, rub my nipples" so I complied. It was at this "moment" I discovered the depth of his strength. Strong, soft, hard and tender all wrapped up in his caramel color exterior.

Noble leans up, hugs me tightly, then kisses me so passionately as his way of thanking me for waking him up the right way. He opens my mouth with his lips and begins sucking my tongue to pull me closer to him. He takes his hand and grabs my hand and puts it in my pants. Our hands are rubbing my sweet muscle together. He then guides my finger to feel the wetness of my own sweet muscle. He knows how much I love to be fingered. I really prefer that it is done more often. My best climax is when I am fingered from behind. It's something about the way that makes me feel. He whispers to me while sucking my neck and kissing my face.

"Take your hand out and taste it then share it with me. Then put it back in there. I want to feel you make love to yourself with your finger until it's dripping from your own excitement."

"Is this my build up for you? To then lick this sweet muscle and sucking on my click. Before you can, take your tongue and lick the opening of my cushion."

He continues kissing me making it hard for me to tell him what I need to happen. But I stay persistent and finish what I'm saying. "I need you to flick your tongue against my opening then lick this sweet muscle again and again while you insert your finger in my cushion to send me to the top of my release."

He takes my hand out my pants and licks every one of my fingers, sucking them so hard. This right here is doing it for me.

"Babe, I need to hit that spot that drives you mad. Take these pants off better yet, I'm taking them off."

And he does exactly that! He is straddling me pulling my pants down while I rub on his chest. It happened so fast that I blinked and now I'm feeling the cool breeze of the A/C. He stops and stares at me with that Duchenne smile. He falls over to the other side of the bed and grabs at the waistband of his pants and I move to straddle him while he does it.

He says, "Nope" with that Duchenne smile and say, "It's me tonight.

You had your turn yesterday," and gently lays me back down.

I notice his pants were removed and he is straddling me once again. He slides down to the end of this bed using his tongue as his marker, drawing a straight line down my body. He stops at my navel drawing a deep sensual penetrating circle right there. I'm twisting, turning, and moving because I need to escape but he grips my soft pillows squeezing them softly then firmly pulling

Tuesday

on their buttons with a slight pinch of his fingertips. He rubs my
legs, pushing them as far apart as they will go. Now I am losing
so much of my bodily juices and this man is quaffing it up like
it's a happy hour at the bar. I feel the instrument in his mouth
pushing in and out, out and in, in and out. For me to say I'm ready
for his true entrance makes me undermine what Noble is doing to
me. I'm gasping for air and begging for him to give it all to me at
the same time. I'm telling myself, "I can handle this, keep it
together. Remember Virgie, his goal is to drive you wild. He is
definitely doing the things he set out to do! It is working in his
favor." Then I grab hold of my pillows and squeeze them tightly
pulling on my own buttons. It is without notice I feel the thrust of
him inside of me hitting my special spot. Thrust after thrust after
thrust slow then fast, then back slow then fast until he has
reached the desired speed he was seeking.

He whispers, "Tell me what you are feeling?" But I can't
speak with the speed of this pace.

He asks again, "Tell me what you are feeling?" But I am still
without words.

His speed intensifies and he yells "Tell me what you're
feeling," and I yell "Fuck!"

He grabs me and turns me over so he can hit this spot from
behind. He places his palms firmly against my cushion. I meet
him with every thrust and allow for the feeling of this fuck to
permeate through my body.

He whispers as we are bent over in this position, "Baby you
have to release so you can be free. Let go of all this stuff that is
holding you back from love, be free with me."

Thrusting again and again as he talks to me. It is at this
moment about maybe four thrusts in that I pushed out everything
I am holding inside.

I collapse under him. I let the tears fall from my eyes.

As we lay there recovering from it all he says, "You know,
you're stuck with this kind of loving so I'll let you know now
you will need to work on strengthening your legs so you're ready
for nights like this." We laugh and cuddle until we fall asleep.

My legs are killing me. Noble is right I have to start back
working out.

I feel like my Auntie when she tells me, "Child this man is trying to kill me."

It's early so I should get in the shower before he wakes up. Damn, I don't have any clean clothes to put on for work. I don't want to wash clothes. Maybe Noble can drive me home so I can grab more clothes to keep over here. Wait a minute, how long am I staying? I miss my place, but I can stay a couple more days for Noble. He wants me to stay forever. Forever, I can't believe I'm thinking it.

I wake Noble and say, "Baby I need to go home and get some clothes for work. I have basically worn everything I have over here." He says, "Okay, do you want to go now? What time is it?"

"It's 6:14." The sun is shining through the blinds.

"Okay I'm getting up now." I notice that Noble is a little stiff and groggy while he is talking to me. I point it right out to him.

"I guess we will both start working on our legs."

"Yeah whatever Ms. Lady, I'm just tired since it's early in the morning."

"Oh okay, I think not," I replied, and we both laugh.

We were up, dressed, and walking out the door within minutes. There wasn't any traffic, so we got to my place very quickly. It felt strange walking back in the building I haven't been in since Saturday. I see a couple of my neighbors who are early morning people. Mr. Corine walks up to us and says, "Virgie I have been wondering what happened to you. Last, I saw or heard anything from you was on Friday when I saw you standing on your balcony in the rain." No need to check temperatures, we were seen out there getting it in oh well.

"Yes Mr. Corine, I decided to stay downtown for the weekend. What happened around here?"

This man is so nosey. I looked at Noble and we both smiled knowing exactly what he was talking about.

Mr. Corine says, "There is a new guy on the 9th floor, and he dates a lot of women. Some of them are attractive and others just let me say I wouldn't date them. Well, he was up there with the dark skin lady and some other light skin lady came over. I think he wasn't expecting her, but those ladies got into an argument. They were standing there calling each other names."

He goes on to say, "The light skin lady left but came back with two guys. One of the guys was banging on the door and when the new guy opened the door one of the two guys punched him in the face and then the new guy pulled out a gun and started shooting."

"Did you tell the police what happened Mr. Corine?"

"Hell no, I'm not getting in that. I live on the 6th floor."

"Did anyone get hurt?"

"Yeah Ms. Virgie, the dark lady that stayed was shot in the arm and one of the two guys was hit in the buttocks as he ran away."

"Mr. Corine, how did the woman get shot if the guy she was in the house with was the person shooting?"

"Oh, I forgot to mention the light skin woman was also shooting into the apartment."

"Wow!" That's why my family was blowing up my phone.

"So, Virgie, are you back or are you leaving again?"

"I'm back just going to work Mr. Corine."

"Have a great day!" He is the nosiest neighbor I ever had. He is way too nosey for me.

"Virgie, why did you lie?"

"Because I don't like people knowing my comings and goings. You see how nosey he is by the story he told us. Either way it goes, I'm sure he will be watching my door or my balcony for any traffic." I start laughing, but Noble didn't think it was funny.

I start grabbing anything I could find so we could get out of there. I'm not sure why I am rushing to leave, but I have this urge to get going.

"Virgie, why are you rushing? What's your urgency?"

"I have no idea. I guess hearing Mr. Corine tell the story about the shooting made me quite anxious."

"Do you know the new guy on the 9th floor?"

"No, I may have seen him, but I can't specifically recall."

"Babe, what about the women he described?"

"I can't say I do."

"Well, you are safe. Take your time. Gather your things. I'll make breakfast. We'll eat and then I'll drop you off to work."

"Okay, you will have to use your master chef skills to make a meal out of the food I have in there."

"Babe, just leave the cooking up to me, we will be okay."

"If you say so Mr. Noble. How many outfits should I bring over to your place?"

"Ms. Lady you will have to figure that out on your own."

"Then I will bring one and come home tomorrow."

"What?" He is about to lose his mind.

"I knew you didn't mean what you were saying?" I laugh. As I walk into the room, I notice Noble is pretty quiet.

"Noble, what are you cooking?" I ask and he doesn't say a word.

"Noble, do you hear me talking to you?" Still nothing. I walk back into the kitchen and see he's passed out on the floor.

I immediately grab him and try to wake him. I need to Call 911. I need to call the paramedics. I grab my cell phone out of my purse on the counter.

"Hello, I have an emergency. I have a black male aged 44 who passed out on the floor. We need the paramedics. I don't know of any medical conditions he has. We are at 1913 S. Madison Street apartment #614.

Hurry please!"

"Noble, paramedics are on the way." I'm crying, praying, and rocking him in my arms.

"Noble, don't leave me please don't leave. You are going to be ok. Baby, don't leave me."

I hear a knock at the door and rush to open it thinking it's the paramedics. But it's not the paramedics, it's Mr. Corine.

He says, "I was in the lobby and forgot to tell you." I scream at him, "Not now something is wrong with my boyfriend and I'm waiting on the paramedics."

Mr. Corine pushes past me and runs to check Noble's pulse. He grabs his wrist to check for a pulse and stare off to the side.

Mr. Corine says, "Virgie. he has a pulse and is still breathing. What happened?"

I begin telling him how I was in the room and now the paramedics are on the scene. They immediately check Noble's vitals and say to me that everything is good. There are two paramedics on the scene male and female and the male grabs a stick out of the medic bag and places it underneath Noble's nose. Noble jumps up ready to fight. Mr. Corine and I start shouting with excitement to see him finally moving.

The paramedics continued checking his vitals then asked if he wanted to go to the hospital to be further checked out.

Noble says, "No, I will be okay."

"Noble, you should go, you had me pretty scared."

"Baby, I'm good I'm sorry I frightened you. I'm just fatigued. I'm good, I don't need to go to the hospital."

Mr. Corine says, "Man you need to go see a doctor."

Noble says, "Sir I am a doctor. I will be fine. Thank you, you fine healthcare professionals I apologize for taking your time away from people who are really in need of your service. It is my hope that no one had an emergency that could not be treated because of me."

"Really!" Now this damn man is over here acting like the Oscar goes to, what just happened? I'm tired all the time and have been extremely tired ever since I have been dating him and I have never passed out. Why is he passing out? There is something wrong with him and as soon as these people clear out of here, he better start talking. The paramedics say that his blood sugar is low, and he should take something. He reveals that he has been stressing and failed to take his medicine. Medicine? He takes medicine. When? For what? Is he serious? What the hell? For how long? Why didn't I know this? Is this why he wants me to move in?

Everyone has cleared out of my apartment and it's just us. Noble is laying on the couch. I walk over to him after escorting everyone out. "Noble, is there anything I can get for you?"

"No baby, I'm okay."

"Noble, you are not okay and stop telling me what you think I need to hear. Why would you not tell me that you're taking medication? Were you scared I would leave you? What is wrong with you? Have you passed out before? What stress are you under?"

"Virgie, I need you to slow down so I can answer your questions one at a time. Come here and lay next to me." I feel so bad he is really sick, and I'm not used to seeing him like this. I start crying.

"Come here baby."

So, I walk towards the couch and he tries to sit up which makes me run over there because I feel like he is not strong enough to be doing that.

"Noble, lay down."

I extend my hands out to push him back down. He grabs me and pulls me to him hugging me tightly.

"I'm okay baby, you are so predictable. I knew if you saw me struggling you would run over here," then he kisses me in my mouth.

Now, I'm sitting on his lap and his head was buried in my chest.

"I'm so sorry I frightened you, Virgie. The last thing I have ever wanted was to make you worry and be frightened for me."

"Noble, what's wrong? How long have you known that you were ill? I am having a hard time with what just happened, and I don't have a clue how I can care for you if you will not be honest with me."

"Virgie I was diagnosed with type 2 diabetes last month."

"What?" He can't be serious. Diabetes, no! He has diabetes. Noble has type 2 diabetes. He is sick. I mean really sick. Why?

"Baby, are you okay? You are not saying anything."

"I'm in shock. You have diabetes! When were you going to tell me? Why would you keep that information from me? I love you and share everything about my life with you."

"Baby, I wasn't keeping it from you." I give him the "yes the hell you were" look.

"Well, I guess I was keeping it from you and I'm sorry. Last month, my body was giving me the impression that something was wrong. It is because I'm a doctor I truly adhere to my body, the signs, and symptoms. I made an appointment and had some tests taken. The results revealed in layman's terms that my blood sugar was too high and needed something to help lower it. I'm on a medication called Biguanides which I take only once a day first thing in the morning with my meal."

"Noble, where are these pills? I have never even seen an aspirin in your place."

"They are in my dresser drawer, on my side of the bed."

"So why Noble?"

"Virgie, I didn't say anything because I haven't fully acknowledged my diagnosis. I have been telling myself that if I take care of myself, eat right, exercise, and get the proper rest I will beat this thing. I normally take my medicine and yesterday I was going to get my prescription filled after I dropped you off to work, but after speaking with you on the phone it escaped me to take my medicine. The day got away from me because it took on a life of itself one thing after the other. I didn't eat anything. I was so worried about you. I thought I lost you yesterday until you called. I didn't come and pick you up because I was feeling lightheaded then."

"Why?" Why am I just hearing about this diagnosis? If it was me, I would have informed him immediately after I received the news.

"Babe you can ask why all night, but it will still remain the same. I didn't tell you about it. So, let's move forward. Not eating yesterday, worrying about us, you, and then getting up so early and not eating food this morning. Even though I did eat something," then he starts rubbing in between my legs. He is smiling too hard trying to be coy.

Before I knew it, I grab his face and say, "Be serious, this is serious!"

He says while still being coy, "I am serious, okay, real serious okay."

"Noble!" I wanted to smack his hand but to be honest, the rubbing did feel good. Real good too!

Noble explains to me that type 2 diabetes can be maintained with healthy eating, exercise and medication management. I feel better now but I also feel awful that I allowed Kelle to send me off which in turn stressed him out.

"Noble, I'm sorry." I feel like shit. He passed out because of me and my baggage.

"For what?" He knows for what, but I have to own up to my shit.

"For all of it." There, I said it.

"All of what?" He knows "what" but okay I messed up, so I just need to tell him the truth.

"Noble, Kelle called me and told me that he saw you in his restaurant with your friend."

"But I told you that me and Raq went there one day after golfing."

"Yeah, but he didn't mention Raq. He said it was a woman."

"Babe, there was a woman at the table with us."

"What? What are you talking about?" So, there is a bitch! Wow! So, I guess he is a lair too that's probably why he passed out so I wouldn't knock his ass out.

"There was a woman with us, but she was with Raq." Oh, she was with Raq's ass. Oh really?

"Really? Now you want to tell me that the woman was with you all and you forgot to mention when you initially told the story."

"Virgie, Raq and I went to the restaurant, only us. We waited in line, we walked to the table together, we ate together. Raq left me sitting at the table by myself then a woman walked up to the table and said she was meeting Raq there. Raq returned to the table and introduced me to his friend Shenine. Shenine was a young lady and I mean young. It looked like she may even still be in high school. I'm talking about young. They left together and I took an Uber home since I rode with him. I didn't want him to drop me off and be giving that child my address. Babe that is Raq's business not mine."

"Noble, I'm not surprised by Raq behavior. I'm surprised by yours."

"Virgie, you are surprised that I withheld my friends' indiscretions from you. That's his business not mine. What we are not talking about is why would you listen to what your ex-boyfriend said?"

"I wasn't listening to him."

"Excuse me I thought you were saying something about being honest."

"Okay, I went off."

"Yes, you did! Virgie, how does he even know we are dating?"

"Noble, I don't know, but he said that he saw me at your place when we ordered breakfast the other day."

"What? When I got the delivery, it was a young man who delivered the food. It appears I am going to have to have a man-to-man conversation with him."

"Noble, I will deal with it."

"No Virgie, I don't need you to do it. He needs to hear it from me."

"No, Noble let me deal with it."

"Babe, then let me say this, if this man's name comes up in our relationship again there will not be a discussion."

He grabs my face this time and says, "You hear me" then kisses me passionately.

"I hear you!

WEDNESDAY

When I say It felt good to take care of Mr. Noble, it was great. I often think back to a time when I wanted someone to look after me when I was ill. I would meet someone who I would be attracted to but ended up disliking him because our relationship was one sided. I was the only person making it work by taking care of us. This is not the case for Mr. Noble. I like the person he is. He is loyal, caring, considerate, dependable, loving, sexy as hell, a provider, a nurturer and a giver. I am not even going to mention how he has all his teeth, feet without corns, strong, bow legged, thick black curly hair, straight eyes, and a smile that makes your heart drop. I remember one night when we first started dating, we went to a concert basically getting to know each other. I was excited but nervous to be out with him because of how handsome he is. I didn't want women pushing up on him. You know these women out here have no filter. I brought my cousin along because she doesn't play. She will check a bitch before the bitch gets to the end of her sentence.

I tried to warn her that he was gorgeous so when he walked up to us as we were waiting in line she said, "Damn! My God, he is fine as hell!" He heard her too. I was so embarrassed. I remember it like it was yesterday. Noble walked up and introduced himself then said to my cousin, "You are just as gorgeous." She turned bright red. I thought that was nice because he didn't pretend like he didn't hear her. We had the time of our lives. Noble rented a hotel suite so we wouldn't have to drive home, and so we could drink and enjoy ourselves. I thought it was over the top, but my cousin said, "The hell with that we are staying the night in this suite on his ass period."

It was his idea. He made all of the arrangements. The reservations and ordered food for the suite. He paid for valet services and any room service requests. Noble did not leave anything for us to be responsible for. My cousin was so drunk she passed out so Noble and I were in the room alone talking and laughing. We were flirting. He would say something that would make me blush. I would place my finger in my mouth and speak with my eyes. He would smile and rub his face with his hand. We would go back and forth with our nonverbals giving the other person a flirtatious signal. I wanted to fuck him so badly. I was sitting in a chair with my legs clenched together because I didn't have on any panties and if I had stood up, I would have revealed this huge wet spot in between my legs. He was the perfect gentleman too. He stayed his distance and often changed the topic when the flirting got a little risqué. I later learned in our relationship that he too was so aroused and had a similar wet spot on his pants. This man, this man.

Good morning Mr. Noble, I went to your place while you slept and got your medicine. You will not be falling out on me again. I even made breakfast. We have multigrain wheat bread, turkey bacon and sausages, white rice, hash browns and fruit."

"Lady come here!"

I walk over to the side of the bed where he is, and he grabs me. "Who do you think you are talking to? Where did you order this food from?" He says.

"Don't worry Mr. Noble, it's from UberEATS." We both laugh so hard. I would cook, but I need to go to the grocery store.

"Virgie, you should have woken me up. If I had woken up and saw, you were gone I would have lost my mind. Even if you wanted me to stay here while you go next time just let me know. There was a shooting in this building and people were injured because of that incident."

"Mr. Noble, the next time you pass out at my house because you didn't eat or take your meds and I need to run to your place and pick it up I will definitely make sure you know what's going on," I respond sarcastically.

"Okay, Ms. Lady you must be hangry because you're getting me straight early in the morning."

"Well, someone has to do it and I gladly accept that responsibility. Now, get up so you can eat and take your meds."

Noble is laying in the bed and says, "Virgie what time do you want to leave for work? I'll drop you off then head to my place."

"I'm not going in today. I took the rest of the week off. I'll be working remotely."

"Virgie, Why? You don't have to watch me. I'm good. I promise."

"Thanks for promising, but the thought of what happened yesterday has me worrying about you. The feeling I feel will not let me leave you right now." I hear the sound of my doorbell chiming.

"Let me answer the door and you get up so we can eat this beautiful breakfast I prepared for us."

The doorbell chimes again. I ask, "Who is it?"

"It's Mr. Corine, your neighbor." He is saying that like I know another nosey ass Mr. Corine. I open the door and he is standing there with my favorite Dutch apple pie in his hands.

"Oh Mr. Corine, you made this for me?"

"Ms. Virgie yeah, I felt pretty bad about what happened with your friend, so I sent my daughter Mari out last night to get the ingredients."

"I didn't know you had a daughter."

"Yeah, she works at a little breakfast place called Kelle, so she is never home. Not to mention she is dating the owner of the restaurant, so I rarely get to see her."

"Mari? I think I met her this weekend."

"You may have, she doesn't normally work weekends, but is trying to make some extra money."

"I am very familiar with that establishment."

"Well, I just wanted to drop the pie off in case you decide to stay at your friend's house for a couple of days. Tell the doctor I said I hope he takes the doctor's orders and takes it easy."

"What doctor would that be?" Is he trying to say I'm doctoring over here on Noble? This old man better not be acting fresh with me.

"Ms. Kelly cut it out," he says then starts laughing as he walks to his apartment.

Wow, Kelle is dating Ms. Mari and Cheryl is worried about me. She is so stupid that Mari got to be all of 23 or 24. I should have asked Mr. Corine, he would have told me too.

"Virgie, who is at the door?"

"It was Mr. Corine bringing you a Dutch apple pie."

"I don't like Dutch apple pie."

88

"I know ha, ha, ha."

"Babe, that's a shame you got the old man falling for you and you are already taken. Stop flirting with him, he probably was thinking don't wake that man up because now you can be all mine."

"I'm not flirting with him; I'm just being neighborly to my neighbor."

"Yeah ok! He really has it bad for you when he is up baking pie in the early morning hours. It sounds like something I would do. He's smooth with his inquisitive ass."

"Noble, that man is not interested in me. He has a daughter younger than me and I'm sure she wouldn't want her dad messing with my young fine ass. I'm just saying for the record."

"Babe every man wants a young fine ass woman. The problem is you're all mine and that's where the trouble begins." "What?" Now he is talking all gangster.

"Virgie, I'm the trouble they will get! Look, stare, compliment but move your ass around."

"Noble, are you jealous?" I'm hearing a little jealousy walking into the conversation.

"Nope, I just know what I have with your young fine ass and I don't want no one else to know."

Breakfast was delicious. Noble decided to go back to bed. He wasn't as strong as he thought he was. I stayed in the living room working. I have an office, but I like to be in an open space when I am working from home. I am on the phone, computer, video conferencing, and cooking. I was able to go to the store after breakfast for food. I told Noble about it before I left and he said, "Take my wallet, don't spend your money. You promise?"

I reluctantly promised. I don't know what it is about me spending his money. I feel bad when I do it. I was always taught if you take money from a man then he will want something in return. It's not like I'm holding back from him whatever he wants, I give it to him. He is not working and it's one thing to be a doctor but one that isn't working that's another thing. How long does he plan to be on this leave of absence? How much money does he really have? Man, I have questions on top of questions. I can't wait until he is comfortable to talk about them.

Noble did share that he was raised by his grandparents. He said that his parents were pretty young when they had him and his grandmother refused to allow him to be raised by them. He said that he has his mother and sister. His mother lives in Florida and his sister who he supports lives in Atlanta. Noble told me that he gave his sister five years to establish something and after that she will be cut off. He said that their agreement was while he was supporting her that she could not move a man in her home, get pregnant, or get married if the man is not in a position to care for her fully. I asked him if he thought that he was too controlling? He immediately denied being controlling. I asked him why he gave her only five years? He said that he would take care of her for the rest of her life, but he wanted her to start to take care of herself too.

He hoped she would have thought he was serious and make a way for herself. Noble said she was always an independent person so he never even thought she would comply with his requests. He said that he never wanted to ponder the thought of her being out there on her own. He just prayed that she would comply, and it would work out for the best. I also asked him how much time is left on this agreement. He said she was actually in her fifth year and at the end of this month she will be cut off. I asked him if she had a full grasp of what being cut off really means. He told me she does. She found someone who loves her immensely. They want to get married and have children. I wanted to know why he put those strongholds on her instead of encouraging her too just be happy.

Noble said his sister grew up having everything she wanted and when their grandparents died it was hard for her to make it on her own. She asked him to help her get started and because he wanted so much for her, he did just that. She graduated from her university magna cum laude. She is a senior executive of a Fortune 500 company and told me the time she used to get herself together actually worked out for her. She is now debt free. He said he didn't even know if it would work but he took a chance on her and would do it all over again.

It's 7:19 pm and Noble is still sleeping. He got up to eat something but went back to bed. I'm glad I stayed home because what would he have done if I was at work. I'm going to take a quick shower and take myself to bed but first I will have a glass of wine and unwind. Today has been a long day. Let me play a little music. I'm standing in the kitchen reaching up in the cabinet when I feel Noble hugging me from behind.

"What are you doing out of bed?

"Babe I came to get you because I'm all rested."

"Whatever Mr. Noble!"

"What is Ms. Lady doing?" I am trying to have some "me" time, but he doesn't understand.

"I'm getting me a glass of wine to unwind before my shower."

"Do you mean before our shower?" I never said "our."

"You were not invited." I'm trying to unwind; he is the one well rested. It's my turn.

"Ms. Lady, I don't need an invitation to shower with my woman."

"Oh really?" The hell he doesn't, this shower is not like his. He needs permission.

"Yes, babe really!" He wins again, I'm too tired.

He turns me around so I'm facing him and kisses me, but it's something about the way he is biting my lips and sucking my tongue that is so arousing. It could be this music that's setting the mood. No, it's him! Yeah, it's him being all well rested.

"Virgie, are we ready to shower?"

"No, I told you I wanted to have a glass of wine and unwind first."

"Well babe, since you have been taking such good care of me, have a seat and I will bring you your wine so you may unwind Ms. Lady."

"Well thank you Mr. Noble, I'll do just that."

I was going to sit in my comfy chair, but I could feel he was feeling a little freaky talking about us taking a shower. When he is feeling freaky, I should sit on the couch because I don't know what he is planning. Noble pours me a glass of dessert wine, he fills the glass like I am a wine connoisseur. I am definitely not. I just like what I like, and it happens to be a dessert wine that was introduced to me by my sorority sister.

Noble walks over to me holding my glass of wine and says, "Why are you sitting on the couch? I just knew you would sit in your chastity chair."

"Really chastity chair? You are crazy!" I say while shaking my head at him.

"Wow, you are truly well rested because you got jokes."

"Virgie, you have to admit it was funny."

"It wasn't funny." It was but since it was about me, I dare not admit it.He has the nerve to be laughing. I guess he cracks himself up. After he hands me my wine, he sits down on the couch then lays his head in my lap. Here we are, in the silence of the room again when Noble begins to talk with the music playing in the background.

"Babe, I just want to "sleep" and not just any "sleep" but to "sleep" with you wrapped all around me. I want to lie next to you and have you "sleep" in my arms, never letting you go. I want to feel the softness of your skin touch the roughness of mine. I don't ever want to "sleep" in a bed while you are in another room away from me. I want to "sleep" while my hands grab the fullness of your pillows and gently squeeze them, so they feel how much I care. I want to collapse in your embrace.

I want to "sleep" alongside you, have you "sleep" on top of me, or "sleep" underneath my arm all night long. I want to rub your cushion up and down then on and against my muscle every night we are together. I want to "sleep" knowing you are delighted to have me "sleep" over. I want to "sleep" so close that I can feel your heartbeat and bounce to its rhythm. I want to "sleep" as I trace the frame of your body with my fingertips not from what I see but from the memory I have stored in my mind. I want to fall straight to "sleep" after I have used my wet tongue leaving my mark of where I have been all over your body. I always want to "sleep" after I have invaded all of your holes first with my tongue, then by my instruments, and finally with my muscle. I love going to "sleep" knowing that even though we did so much that there is so much more we can do. I want to "sleep" with you, so I ask, "Do you really want to go to "sleep?""

"Yes! Noble, I want to go to sleep."

"What Virgie? Are you serious? After everything I just described to you, you really want to go to sleep."

"Noble, I want to sleep, but only after you do what you just said you want to do."

"Well babe, I guess it's bedtime!"

This man, this man, what can I say about this man? I am worn out and he is too. He is over there fast asleep after doing everything he wanted to do to me. So why am I not sleeping? I don't have a clue, oh yeah, I have to pee. Let me get up and go to the bathroom before he thinks I'm ready for round two. Too late, I can hear Noble.

"Baby is everything okay? Did I hurt you?"

"Noble I'm fine, I will be right there."

I should stay locked up in this bathroom. I can't take it anymore. I need just a good night's "sleep." No cuddling, no kissing, and no fucking.

I'm tired and my legs are weak. I hear him knocking at the door.

"Are you okay?"

"Yes, I'm good can a lady have a moment to herself?"

"Sure, it's just that I have to urinate."

"Noble, you can go to the other bathroom?"

"Of course, I could Virgie! I just didn't want you to think I left."

"Noble, go to the other bathroom."

I could hear him walking into the guest room. I love him, but I am tired, and sleep deprived. After being single for so long, this is not really a bad thing. Shut up Virgie, just shut up is what I say in my head.

I was right round two, here we go again. I walk back to bed and discover Mr. Noble has removed all of his clothes.

He says to me, "Remember I want to feel the softness of your skin against mine?"

"I remember you said that, but I thought you were just talking. Noble, I'm tired, can we just go to sleep?"

"Yes, just don't get in bed with those clothes on though."

Why am I doing this? I should go to sleep in the guest room but no I am standing right here getting in bed without clothes, even though I like to sleep fully clothed. The A/C is blasting which makes it a little chilly in here too. Noble is laying in the bed holding the blanket up while I crawl my ass between the sheets and blanket. I have to cuddle with him just to warm up, but I know this is not a good idea.

Surprisingly, he is actually behaving. If anything, it is me who is all hot and bothered from this cuddling. I could feel his muscle regaining its strength and becoming hard and strong while I'm laying here. I can feel my sweet muscle fully awake and pulsating. A matter of fact, she is quite moist. Mr. Noble is not budging. It was as if he knew what I said to myself in the bathroom. I look him in the face, and he is fast asleep again. He has me in this bed naked and he is actually asleep. I really can't stand him, now I want to fuck, and he is asleep. Wow! I'm going to sleep too.

THURSDAY

I am awakened by a familiar chiming, but I can't make out what it is. I have Noble sprawled all over my bed and on me. There is this chiming sound again, oh I know what it is, it's my cellphone. What time is it?

Where is my phone? I don't have an alarm on it so why is it making this sound? Why is it ringing? There it is on the table.

"Natasha Janine, why are you doing this damn FaceTime stuff? What time is it?" She knows I hate looking at people to talk on the phone.

"Girl, it's 8:14 am. I have been trying to reach you all morning." Really, I didn't even hear my phone maybe because I was "unwinding with Noble."

"Why, what happened?" Let me brace myself.

"Twaab was rushed to the hospital." Oh my God!

"What? What happened?" Please Lord let her be okay, please!

"We were in a car accident." I repeat the words, "a car accident!" How?

Who was driving? I have so many questions.

"Oh my God! What hospital are you all at?"

"We are at Northside Hospital."

"We? You were with her? Where is Dominica?"

"Dominica just arrived. I have called both of you all morning."

"Are you okay?" I'm so worried about my sister; I didn't ask about her.

"Yes, I have minor injuries, but they are still working on your sister."

Lord, what does she mean "working on my sister?"

"Natasha Janine, I'm on my way. Let me wake Noble, I will see you soon. Did you call MJ too?"

"No, I didn't." Why didn't she call MJ? She knows that MJ should be the first person called if something happens in my family.

"Why not?" This must be really bad.

"Never mind, I'll call her and have her meet me there." I'm not going to deal with this with just Dominica. I need my big sister and I definitely need her praying. I end FaceTime and wake Noble.

"Noble, I need to go to the hospital. Twaab was in a car accident."

"Virgie, what happened?"

"I don't know, but she was with Natasha Janine and they had an accident. Natasha Janine has some minor injuries, but they are working on Twaab."

"Babe, I will make some calls and get some information. I worked there; don't worry she is being treated by some of the best hands in medicine. Get dressed so we can get out of here."

We are dressed and headed into the garage to get the car. Damn, I need to call MJ. I dial her number as we are walking to the car.

She answers and I say, "Hey sister! Twaab was in a car accident. I don't have any details other than she was with Natasha Janine. Natasha Janine has minor injuries and Twaab is being worked on now at Northside hospital. Dominica is there and Noble and I are on our way. We should be there in 15 minutes. Okay, I will see you then. Love you sister and be careful."

We are in the car and Noble looks over at me and says, "Babe you got me distracted."

"What are you talking about?"

"Virgie, you know I love it when you wear those jogging pants."

"What? Can you keep your head on straight?"

"Babe that's why I am telling you because my head is straight so I'm going to need a minute before I get out of this car."

"Are you serious?" I ask in disbelief.

"Babe, what do you think?" I looked and he was not lying; he is at full attention. This man, this man!

"Noble, drop me off at the door and park the car so you can get yourself together." I'm shaking my head! What am I going to do with him?

We pull up at the entrance and I see Natasha Janine and Dominica. Dominica runs up to me crying.

Thursday

I ask, "What's wrong? What happened? Is she ok? Why are you crying?"

Dominica says, "She is fine. I'm happy you are here. You know I can't stand Natasha Janine's ass and I had to talk to her the whole morning." Ever since Dominica was arrested last year and Natasha Janine defended her in court Dominica hates her. Dominica was mad that she had to plead to probation and thinks that Natasha Janine didn't do her job. I have explained to her that Natasha Janine did the best she could do with her case. Dominica drove into a crime scene that was closed to traffic and hit a pole. The incident was caught on several body-worn cameras and by several squadrons. For some reason she thinks Natasha Janine could have proven it wasn't her, this woman is crazy.

"Girl shut up! We are here for Twaab."

Natasha Janine has her arm in a sling and some bruises on her face.

I ask her, "Are you okay?"

"Yeah Virgie, I'm fine."

Then I walk over to Dominica who walked over to the other side of the emergency room door. "Dominica, why didn't you call MJ?"

"Because Virgie, she is always praying and preaching to me. How was I going to tell her that her sister Twaab is fucking around with your friend?"

"What?" This lady has truly lost her mind.

"Virg stop playing like you didn't know they were messing around?"

"No, I didn't." I would have never even considered that Natasha Janine loves men.

"Well, Twaab's ex-girlfriend saw them driving around this morning and crashed into them."

"What?" Here she goes, saying something that I will have to figure out later.

"Yes sister, it's fucked up and I'm going to fuck her up when I see her too! That's some dirty shit she did."

Now, I know that there is a little truth to this story, but I'm going to have to figure it out later. I need to find out what happened to Twaab.

Noble walks into the waiting room. You would think he is Denzel Washington or somebody. These women are running around like he is all that, which he is, but I don't like it. One lady walks up to him and says, "Dr. Winston, we missed you. How are you? When are you coming back? Things aren't the same since you left."

I walk up and grab his hand. He turns and kisses me and asks, "Are you okay babe?"

"I'm fine baby, but I don't know what's happening with Twaab."

"Nurse Avery, can you tell Dr. Tapes? I'm here," I see they have some history because he knows her personally.

She says, "I sure will."

Dr. Tapes is his friend who he helped the other day. I didn't know he works here. I walk to the area where Natasha Janine and Dominica are sitting with Noble.

"Who the hell is this?" Dominica asks.

"Dominica, this is Noble, my grown man!" I bet she doesn't even remember what she said about him.

Noble and I start laughing and he says, "Hello Dominica it is my pleasure to meet you. I'm just sorry we are meeting during this unfortunate circumstance."

She asks him, "Why did you say that? Did they say my sister died?"

"Dominica! Cut it out!" She is always overreacting.

"Sister, tell him to cut it out, he is the one talking about unfortunate circumstance shit, and what the hell does that mean anyway?"

"Dominica, he is talking about being in an emergency room setting."

"Awe man, why didn't you say that dude?"

"Your right young lady, it was quite insensitive of me to say at this time."

"It's just Dominica."

"Okay girl, he got it."

Noble turns and says, "Hello Natasha Janine. I'm sorry to hear you were injured. How are you feeling?"

"I'm fine just worried about Twaab."

"Natasha Janine, my friend is the attending physician here and he will give us some information soon. Is there anything I can get for you?" This is Noble's attempt to change the tone of the conversation.

"No, I'm good and thanks for asking."

Dominica looks at her and rolls her eyes. She is too much.

MJ comes running up and Dominica puts her head down as does Natasha Janine. MJ is not paying attention and runs right into Noble's back as he is standing next to me. Noble turns around and MJ says, "My God!" Then she clinches her pearls.

"I'm so sorry, excuse me sir."

MJ knew I was dating Noble, but only talked to him over the phone. She has never actually seen him. I walk over and give her a hug and she say, "I see why we can't get in touch with you oh my."

I laugh and she goes to hug Dominica. "Hello sister I haven't seen you in a while."

"Yeah, you know that's on purpose." Dominica is so silly. She always has something smart to say especially to MJ.

"Well, I'm still praying for you," says MJ.

MJ then walks over to Natasha Janine and says, "I hear you were hurt also I pray you feel better soon."

Yeah, I think Dominica may be right because Twaab tells MJ everything and I mean everything and the way she is treating Natasha Janine tells me something is definitely wrong with this picture. Noble interjects my thoughts and says, "I get to meet the whole family."

Dr. Tapes then walks out. Natasha Janine gives me "he's fine" side eye and I reply with "yes he is" side eye back at her.

Noble introduces Dr. Tapes to Natasha Janine and Dominica. He did not introduce him to MJ because she walked into the chapel to pray. Noble says, "You remember Virgie."

"Noble, I wouldn't forget her." I'm standing up here with my flirtatious ass looking at him with my big round eyes.

"Yeah, I'm the woman you can't forget." Noble looks at me like "cut it out now." So, I stop it right there, he doesn't like that.

Dr. Tapes says, "I want to let you all know that Ms. Kelly is doing fine. She has multiple fractures to her legs, contusion to her chest, and several broken toes. She is alert and is asking for her..."

I ask, immediately interrupting him as he is speaking, "Me?"

He replies, "No, she is asking for her sister..."

I interrupt him again, "Oh, that's my oldest sister, MJ?" She definitely wants to talk to MJ.

He then says, "No, she asked for her younger sister. I think she said, Donna."

"Dominica! She is asking for Dominica, wow!" He could not be serious. Dominica, wow!

"Yawl just knew she wanted to see yawl asses and it's me she wants to see," Dominica says to me and starts laughing as she walks to the back to see Twaab.

Natasha Janine says, "I can't believe she doesn't want to see me." I grab her by the arm and drag her straight outside of the door.

I ask Natasha Janine, "When did you start dating my sister?"

"What? I'm not dating your sister!"

"Yes, you are!" She might as well tell the truth everybody in my family knows now.

"Virgie how are you going to tell me who I am dating, I am not dating you sister. Why do you think that I am because we were in the car together?"

"Dominica told me that you all are dating."

"Virgie, Dominica doesn't know a damn thing and I know she is your sister."

"Then why? Why were you and her driving around late at night?"

"She and I are friends. I think you should speak to Twaab about what she was doing. It is not my business to disclose," she says.

"Natasha Janine, what the hell are you talking about? You tell me because you are my friend."

"Virgie, your sister is in love with me, and I don't see her like that. She called me to pick her up and while in the car she grabbed a hold of my steering wheel and crashed my car."

"What? My sister grabbed your steering wheel and crashed your car."

"Yes Virgie. I told her that I was in love with a woman and for some reason she thought it was her because we spend so much time together. I'm not gay but I have found myself attracted to a woman but only that woman."

"What Natasha Janine? How are you not gay if you are attracted to a woman?"

"It's complicated and you need to talk to your sister."

Natasha Janine walks back into the hospital, but I remain standing outside. What woman is she attracted to? Why is this the first time I'm hearing this?

Noble walks up to me and says, "Are you ok?"

"No, I'm not, I need to talk to Twaab. I need to talk to her now."

Twaab is lying in the bed with her leg in a sling, bandages on her feet, and bruises on her face and head. I walk in and say, "Hey sister!"

"Hey sister, I know I was acting stupid."

"Yes, you were Twaab. What is going on?"

"Well, I went out with some friends drinking. Things took a turn for the worst when my guy Zam started arguing with this guy in the bar and they got into a fight. The police were called so I got out of there. I called Natasha Janine to come and get me. She got there and started talking to me about my friends and I was too aggressive for her. So, I asked, "What does that mean?" She went on to say, loving us is too complicated. I asked her to explain, and she started talking about how she would never date a woman and I told her she was a lie. We started arguing and she kept dismissing me. I grabbed the steering wheel to get her attention and we crashed into a light pole on my side of the car."

"Twaab, are you in love with her?"

"Virgie, why do you ask that?"

"Dominica said something about yawl being together. I know we have to piece things together to get the truth out of Dominica's conversation but when you asked for her to come in the room before any of us. I knew right then that there was more to this story."

"Virg, there is no more!"

"You are lying. Natasha Janine is lying, and Dominica doesn't even know where the lie is in all of this. Twaab, are you going to make me ask MJ who I know is not going to lie? You tell her everything and I know she knows what's happening here."

"Virg, there is nothing more to know."

"Okay, if that's what you are saying."

"Let's talk about something else, Noble used to be a physician here."

"Yeah, I know."

"How do you know?"

"Dr. Tapes told me. He said we have a very important friend in common and I said who and he told me it was Noble."

"Twaab, I hope you didn't say..."

She interrupts me while I am speaking and say, "Well I did, I said with his sweet ass."

"Twaab, please tell me you are lying?" How do you say that to someone's friend?

"Nope, I said exactly that, and he laughed and told me that I was totally wrong. He said he is as straight as they come. Dr. Tapes said he hopes my sister doesn't break his heart because he can't take another heartbreak."

"What did he mean by that?" I am curious to know.

"I asked him, and he wouldn't say, but he did say no one ever thought he would ever try it again."

"Try what?" What is it that Noble would never try again?

"Virgie, its Love! Can you send MJ in here?" Noble did say that to me. Something had to happened.

"Twaab, you don't want to see Natasha Janine?"

"Nope I'm good. Yawl can go home. They will begin admitting me and I'm going to talk to MJ and have her pray then rest up from all these meds they are giving me. Virgie, Thanks for coming, love you."

"Love you too Twaab!"

I walk back into the waiting room and I see Noble sitting next to Dominica in tears laughing. I told him he would like her.

MJ asks, "How is she?"

"She is good, and she wants to see you." MJ immediately starts walking back towards Twaab's room. Natasha Janine appears to be distraught.

"What's wrong girl?" I ask her.

"Virgie, so I guess she doesn't want to see me, does she?"

"No, she asked if everyone could leave and come back tomorrow."

"Well, can you all give me a ride back to my place?"

"Of course, we can Natasha Janine."

Dominica says, "Me too because I'm not riding with MJ. I think she was sprinkling water on me because I kept feeling water against the back of my neck and whenever I would turn and look at her, she would turn her head. She knows what she was doing. I will walk home before I ride with her." We all burst out laughing.

Dominica then asks, "Why the hell are yawl laughing? I'm serious that damn girl is touched."

"Well, let's wait for MJ to come out before we leave."

MJ is our oldest sister. She raised us after our mother died. Our grandparents were our guardians and when they both died, we were very young. We went to live with our mother. Our mother was the fun mom, so everyone came to visit us. We had little to no guidance, but MJ immediately changed that. She started cooking, cleaning, getting us to school, and made all of us including my mother go to church. MJ's name is really Marion but because she is named after our grandmother, we all called her Marion Junior (MJ). She was our everything growing up. She and Dominica have this love hate relationship because of Dominica's life choices. Dominica is a fun girl like our mother which makes us worry too often about her. She is young and impressionable. MJ wants her to change her ways and she keeps praying that one day she will. Dominica is more ashamed of the way she lives than how MJ feels about her. She is the only one of us that has money put away for her future like Noble's sister. Dominica doesn't want to change or be controlled so MJ refuses to sign the money over which forces her to take care of a grown ass woman. MJ can't make Dominica follow any rules or expectations, so she basically acts as Dominica's payee.

Twaab has always needed more attention. MJ has always made sure she was treated extra special. I know Twaab is back there telling MJ what really happened. Any of us can talk to MJ about anything and she will not pass any judgment against us. Dominica and I hold her in high esteem, so we don't share much of our lives unless we have too. Twaab is her favorite. I mean bestie. MJ will deny it if she is asked but we know the truth. Twaab shares everything with MJ. So, I'm just going to have to get the details from MJ since I am only getting half-truths from Natasha Janine and Twaab. MJ can keep a secret, but I always find a way to get the answers I need from her.

We have been sitting here laughing, sharing and enjoying each other's company for a while when MJ comes out.

She says to me, "Virgie, I need to speak with you?" I get up and walk outside with her.

"MJ, what's wrong?"

She says, "Twaab says you are mad with her."

"I'm not mad at Twaab I just feel like there is more to what happened in this incident and I want to know what's really going on?"

"Well Virgie, just leave it alone for everyone's sake."

"MJ, what are you talking about? Dominica tells me that my best friend and sister are dating. Then Twaab asked for her to come to the back before seeing me or you. Natasha Janine tells me my sister is in love with her and she is in love with another woman. I went to see my sister and she told me this story she was out drinking with Zam who got into a fight and had my best friend pick her up. Now, you are out here telling me to leave it alone. What the hell is going on? I'm sorry for my language but enough already. What are you all trying to keep me from knowing?"

"Virgie, Natasha Janine and Twaab were hanging out quite a bit partying. Twaab started having feelings for her and Natasha Janine told her that they couldn't be together because she has feelings for you."

"What? Natasha Janine has feelings for who?"

"You Virgie! Twaab asked for Dominica because Dominica is the one who told Twaab. Dominica said Natasha Janine told her the only reason she was representing her was because she was in love with her sister." I bust out laughing.

"Virgie, why are you laughing?"

Natasha Janine told me the same thing however she said the only reason I am representing you is my love for your sister not I'm in love with your sister and I continued laughing.

"No Virgie, Dominica has the message on voicemail. Natasha Janine said I'm in love with your sister. She is the one who is not being honest."

"Wow, so what happened in this car accident?"

"Twaab asked Natasha Janine to come get her. She did and they started arguing in the car and Twaab grabbed the steering wheel and crashed."

"So, MJ, you are telling me that my best friend is gay and in love with me?"

"Yes sister! This is exactly what I am telling you." I'm speechless!

Noble and I dropped off Dominica first because she lives closer to the hospital. On the ride to Natasha Janine's house I say, "I need to talk to you. What is your schedule looking like?"

"Virgie, I'm free." I am going over there even if she wasn't free.

"Okay, I will bring breakfast tomorrow and we can talk then." Yeah, because I need some answers.

"Sure, I will see you in the morning. Thanks for the ride." Yeah okay.

I say to add my dig at her, "That's what friends are for." I know she felt my petty dig at her too. I look at Noble and he is looking perplexed about our interaction because we are normally less formal.

We arrived in front of her house and she gets out. "Thanks, Noble, you all try and enjoy the rest of the day."

"You too Natasha Janine," I say before Noble could say anything.

Noble says, "Babe what the hell is going on?"

"What do you mean?" I know he doesn't have a clue of what is happening.

"You know what I mean. Dominica said Natasha Janine is in love with you, but her and Twaab was messing around with each other. Twaab got mad and grabbed the steering wheel and crashed into a pole."

"Noble, are you serious?" Dominica told him the correct details of this nightmare.

"Yes, I'm serious that's what your sister told me." Wow, either I am losing my mind or Dominica has found hers.

I start laughing and say, "Well that is the first time in history that Dominica got the whole story correct without anyone needing to decipher what she is talking about. She has never been able to tell all the facts in the correct order."

"Dominica said you all think she makes up things, but she just changes it around to keep it interesting." I'm dying laughing.

"Noble, Dominica is correct for a change. Everything happened just like that and I can't believe I'm admitting to what Dominica is saying."

Noble starts laughing at himself and says, "Dominica is my favorite sister-in-law."

"Wait one-minute Mr. Noble, we are not married."

"Correction Ms. Lady, not married yet!"

We are at my place in a matter of seconds, really minutes. I walk into my apartment with a head full of thoughts.

"Noble, can we order in? I'm too tired to cook and I don't want you standing over the stove either."

"Sure, what would you like?"

"Chinese! Order me some shrimp egg foo young with extra gravy, shrimp toast, shrimp in black bean gravy sauce, two veggies egg rolls and an order of pan-fried noodles."

"Babe, should I order myself something?"

I walk into the room laughing. I can hear him order everything I asked for, so I turn on the shower. I wish I could wash this day away. My world as I know it is being crushed right before my eyes. And to top it off, Dominica knows exactly what she is talking about. I can't and will never recover from this one right here. I'm happy there is no permanent physical damage to them, and no other parties were involved in this senseless crash. I'm going to have to pay for the damages to Natasha

Thursday

Janine's Porsche SUV because Twaab's broke ass doesn't have the money.

Noble calls me saying, "Babe?"

"Yes Noble?" I know he hasn't forgotten what I asked him to order.

"The food should be here in 30 minutes and I told him if we don't answer that the door is open and to leave it at the entrance because the tip is included."

"What do you mean if we don't answer the door?" Why wouldn't we answer the door if we are expecting a delivery?

"Because I had you go to bed hot and bothered just so I could make love to you this morning. And since we have been out all day, I need to release right now after watching you in those jogging pants all day.

You couldn't imagine how hard it was to make this muscle stay down." I'm over here shaking my head. This man, this man!

Noble walks up behind me and whispers in my ear while kissing the nape of my neck. "After entering this house, all I want to do is have a hot shower. I would like to wash your body. I need you to allow me to drift away as I touch you. Babe, I want to wash your legs, then these thighs that were hugged tightly in those jogging pants. I have to do it slowly and methodically. I want you to tease me like you were doing when you kept walking past me in the hospital. I want you to place my hands where you want me to feel you first. I want you to recall how wet I made you last night and all the things you needed me to do. I want to dip your head over in the shower so the water can roll down the arch of your back. I need you to hold every emotion inside before you are touched by my muscle making me want you even more.

While you are bent over in the water, I want to wash your stomach and then move to wash each one of these pillows," as he is rubbing intensely at my breasts. "I want to slowly then pull your buttons one by one. I want to take that soap and wash your neck and after droplets of water have cleared the soap off then I am going to suck the softness of your skin like this," while he is sucking my neck as an example of what he is going to do.

"I will rub your back with such a delicate kind of touch, the kind of touch that has me moving up and down. I will wash the straight line of your spine. Then, I will lather that towel a little more so that I can wipe your cushion clean from behind and when the lather is cleared away, I will kneel down to catch the water that drops down off this," while gripping my derrière. "I will wash my hands while I am down there so I can take a closer look. I will use my fingers as the instrument to check if the valley of this most important muscle is clean and ready for intruders. When your body is washed oh so delicately, I am going to need you to wash me. I prefer this to occur as I'm inserting these fingers into your opening whichever one, they find first. But if you feel that the cleaning of your body needs to commence then I will continue pushing my fingers in and out making you gasp for air. I will be kissing you and sucking your tongue like you don't want this to ever end."

"Noble, what if the delivery man comes in while we are doing all that?"

"Virgie, I don't give a damn who comes in here just as long as they don't make me stop. Now come on, enough with this narration shit let's make this soliloquy happen."

FRIDAY

Another night of not eating. I knew when I told him to order the food that I would eat it for breakfast. It is as if I knew it would be a great morning meal. We did all of these sensual things in the shower, on the bed, on the floor, and even in my "chastity chair." I don't know if knowing someone else is in love with me made this man ferocious, but this lady right here was well pleased beyond her deepest fantasy. I think every muscle in my body needs a massage. When I say he did it all, oh wee he did it all. Even when I was reciprocal, we had to do it at the same time. He would not stop his pursuit of pleasing me, so he kept using all of his body's instruments entering them in all of my openings while he was receiving pleasure from me. I had to ask myself while we were in the thick of it, ""Can you do this for the rest of your life?" I don't think I can keep this up, but I can say I am willing to try. I think I even heard the delivery person last night, but I was caught up in the moments of screaming, yelling, and cursing so loudly he probably figured out we were here and just too busy to stop.

The food was placed on the counter which is a distance away from the door. They must have stopped, watched, and listened before they left.

I'm correct, the delivery person did. They left this note on the receipt, "I knocked, and no one answered so I took the liberty of placing the food on the counter. I figured you were unavailable. Thanks for the tip!" I hollered and showed Noble when he walked into the living room.

"Babe, I wonder if my skills were rated?" Yep Noble, you would wonder that.

"You know what, I can't with you and your nasty self."

"Virgie, you love everything about this nasty," while pointing to himself. "Say you don't, and you would be lying."

"Whatever Mr. Noble!" I would give you a 10 but I think I would never let me live it down.

"So, you are about to go visit your friend?"

"Yeah, we need to talk." I really need to get to the bottom of this.

"Are you good with this Noble?" Please let him be okay with this. She is family.

"Yes, she's your friend. The question is how are you babe?" Thank goodness, I don't need any more confusion.

"I feel betrayed."

"Babe, I would just hear what she has to say before you think about the whole betrayal piece. People have their reasons for why they are not immediately honest with you."

"What do you mean?" I wonder who these "people" are he is talking about.

"Babe you can be a little judgmental." Me "judgmental" hell no!

"Noble, you think so?" I don't know if he is serious or playing around.

"I know Virgie because the minute someone tells you something negative, you are off to the gallows to cut someone's head off."

"I don't agree with your assessment of me."

"Babe I know you wouldn't, but I say when you talk to her to have an open mind, loving heart and an empathetic ear to hear. And while you are there I'm going to go home. I love it here, but I miss the order my home provides for me."

"Well, this is my home and I have no plans of leaving. If I am to be your wife, then you would live here with me."

"Now babe since you have mentioned it, we probably shouldn't get married." I punch him in the arm so fast, I surprised myself. He then says, "I love you babe and come to the condo when you finish." "Okay will do," then I kiss him before he leaves.

I'm not judgmental and I don't think people think I'm that way. I am going to ask my Auntie; she will tell the whole truth. I should call her while I'm driving to Natasha Janine's house.

"Hey Auntie, I'm calling you from my speaker phone in the car in case it's hard for you to hear me."

"I can hear you! Why didn't yawl asses call me yesterday about Twaab ass being in a car accident?"

"There was so much going on I'm sorry for not calling. Who told you what happened?"

"MJ's ass! She called me talking about Twaab, Natasha Janine and your ass."

"Auntie, she didn't mention Dominica and Noble?"

"Virgie, yeah but they didn't do shit. She just wanted me to know what happened with yawl."

"Yeah, I'm on my way to Natasha Janine's with breakfast."

"Why do you keep feeding that bitch? Bad enough you are going to have to pay for those repairs to her car because you know your sister broke as hell."

"Auntie, she is my best friend."

"Now here you go with that best friend shit."

"How are you this morning?"

"Child, I'm good. Sid just left and worked an old bitch out all night so I'm about to take a bath and get me some ben-gay on these old joints."

"Auntie, do you think I'm judgmental?"

"Child, hell yeah!"

"Why do you say that?"

"Because you are, but I don't pay your ass no attention, so it doesn't bother me."

"Well, Noble told me that and I wanted to see what you think."

"Noble did, did he? Now tell me about this Noble because MJ said he was so damn fine she almost forgot about her religion and had to clinch her pearls." I'm cracking up. MJ did clinch those pearls.

"Virgie Mae, she said he made her clinch her muscle too," and we both are laughing uncontrollably. "If he does all that then I am going to need to see his ass for myself. When am I going to meet him?"

"I hope soon."

"Child don't hope shit. Make it happen for your favorite aunt."

"Okay Auntie, I'll call you later!"

"Okay love you child."

"I love you too!"

I pull up to Natasha Janine's and I see her walking into the house. Where has she been this morning? It's not even 10 o'clock yet. I blow the horn to let her see it is me, so she is aware I'm here. She waves and continues walking inside. I park in her driveway and I notice there are two cars parked there. One of the cars is the car her dad gave her, which is an antique, but the other car I have never seen. Whose car is that? It is a silver Malibu with tinted windows. I get out and grab the food as I'm walking up to the door. I see Mari the waitress coming out of her house. What the hell is she doing here? How does Natasha

Janine even knows her. We met her at the Kelle's restaurant Saturday.

Mr. Corine told me she was dating the owner, but she is over Natasha Janine's house. Oh, hell no! What the hell is going on here?

Mari is leaving fast and says, "Hey Virgie!"

"Hey Virgie? We aren't friends and what are you doing here?" I hear Natasha Janine beckoning me to come inside and leave her alone. I don't know if she answered, but I was giving her the stare down as I was walking in the house. Mari continues to walk away, and I run upstairs to get my questions answered.

"Natasha Janine, how the fuck do you know Mari? What the fuck is going on? What the fuck is happening here?"

"Virgie, I will explain everything, let me get some plates. There is so much going on and I don't know where to start."

Now we are sitting at the table and she has yet to start talking. I'm looking at her like "bitch" and I start talking since she won't, I will. "Girl, are you losing your damn mind? This wouldn't be the first-time smart lawyers went really crazy. Do you need to see a psychiatrist?

What is happening?"

"Virgie, I have fucked up that's what happened!"

"How? When did it all happen?"

"Let me start from the beginning. Remember when I went out with Raq?"

"Yeah, I remember."

"Virg, well wait a minute let me start over. Before you and Noble got together I was coming over to your place a lot, remember?" I actually made you come over because you were acting crazy.

"Okay I remember."

"And I was drinking a little heavy." Girl. "heavy" is an understatement. You were drinking like a horse.

"Okay, would you just tell the story?"

"Well, the reason I was doing so was I got involved with one of my clients." Many lawyers do that, we shouldn't but it happens to the best of us. I dated Kelle's ass.

"Okay?"

"And that client was a female. And I was ashamed of what happened between us." I'm still trying to process this.

"Natasha Janine, would you just tell the damn story?"

"Okay here it is. Albert from law school asked me to take this case. The case was a young lady arrested for domestic battery. He thought I could help her. I contacted the lady who is Mari Corine, the waitress from the restaurant."

"Natasha Janine, you knew her and played like you didn't when we were at the restaurant and let me tip that bitch and that is some lowdown shit."

"Virgie!"

"Okay, I digress, get back to the story." I still can't believe I tipped her ass.

Natasha Janine is sitting here holding her head down fidgeting with her hands and says, "Mari was arrested for domestic battery. I would frequently meet with her about her case. She is a cute girl and I have never been attractive to women before, but I often felt like she was flirting with me. It wasn't until one night when we were meeting, she came over to my place to show me pictures of her partner and what her partner was posting about her on social media. She came looking drop dead gorgeous. You know me always encouraging others. I was complimenting her and was also tipsy. I mean drunk that I started talking really provocatively to her. She started kissing me and next thing I know we were locked in this house for two days."

"Shortly after, I defended her in court and won the case. I would often call her after the case was over and she wouldn't return any of my calls. I started drinking heavily. This is the time when you had started having me come over to your place a lot because you were worried about me. Well, one day I was walking into your building and I heard a voice say hold the elevator please. I knew it was her and it was. She said she was going to visit her dad who lives on the 6th floor. But I instead pushed 9 because I wasn't letting her get away and not explain what happened. She lied of course telling me that she is no good for me and that I wasn't gay that I was just curious. But I remained persistent to get her to explain what happened. I got her to agree to meet me later. She went to see her dad and I met her over my house later that night. We would do this thing for about 2-3 months until that night I went out with Raq."

"What does he have to do with it?"

"Virgie, I was confused, and I thought fucking him would prove I was straight so he asked to have a threesome and I initially said no, but he wouldn't take no for an answer. We were at his place and he called a young lady to come over.

"Natasha Janine, did he call Mari over? What the hell?"

"Virgie, no he didn't."

"Then who did he call over?"

"He called her ex-girlfriend Shenine."

"Get the hell out of here! Shenine is the girl who met Noble and Raq at Kelle's that day they went there. Shenine, wow!"

Natasha Janine continues and says, "Shenine walked into the house and recognized me instantly."

"Get the hell out of here! So, what happened?" I say to myself I need my tea for this as I am taking a sip.

"She felt the need to call Mari to come over too." That nasty bitch, I can't stand her ass already.

"Natasha Janine, shut the damn door, the whole door." I'm about to pass out on this floor.

"Yes! Now Raq was sitting back for the show. Mari got there in a matter of minutes and came in accusing me of sleeping with her ex-girlfriend. Now at this time Mari was the only woman I had slept with. Shenine and Raq start fucking around in front of us. Mari was instantly turned on by this and grabbed my hand and led me over there with them to join in this shit."

"So, Raq is fucking all of yawl?"

"Yes, and we are all doing each other. It was some crazy shit. After that

I didn't want to have anything to do with Raq and I cut Mari's ass off too. I told Twaab what happened and her and I started hanging out. She is the closest gay friend I have so we became besties."

"Is that when you and Twaab started sleeping together?"

"Hell no, really Virgie, I never slept with her."

"What? Are you telling the truth? Or are you really trying to shield my feelings?'

"Virgie, you heard me I never slept with her! That's the reason we had the car accident. When I picked her up, I told her that her friends were too aggressive for me. She told me that she loved me and asked me if I loved her. I told her she was like a little sister to me and that I have feelings for only one woman. She then grabs my steering wheel talking about "bitch you in love with my sister" Dominica told me. I was telling her to let go of the steering wheel and within seconds we crashed into the light pole."

"Dominica told Twaab that you left a message on her phone saying you were in love with me."

"Bitches are you for real? Virgie, I can't stay in a hotel room with your messy ass. And Virg, you believed that shit? Really! Girl, hell no! Dominica's crazy ass asked me to ask the judge if she could pay him to keep her from serving probation and I told her if I didn't love your sister, I wouldn't even be representing your ass."

"So, you didn't leave a message on her phone saying this."

"Really Virgie, you know your damn sister is crazy. No, I didn't leave a message on her phone. To be perfectly honest, I didn't even have her number back then Twaab was my go-to person when I was working on her case."

"Girl, I'm so glad you are not in love with me."

"Hell, me too!"

"So, Natasha Janine tell me why Mari is back in the picture."

"Virg, again after that night with Raq, I cut their asses off for real. So, when we walked into Kelle's restaurant, she walked up to the table. I could have died. I hadn't seen her in about two months. She is the reason why I stopped visiting you. I didn't want to bump into her ass or see her old nosey ass daddy. She called me after we left the restaurant talking about, we needed to talk so I said okay. She told me that she got an apartment in your building with her boyfriend on the 9th floor and her dad doesn't know anything about it. She asked me to meet her on the 9th floor so we can talk. When I get there and knock on the door and this ugly ass guy comes to the door asking me all these damn questions. I turned to walk away, and she came out the apartment running up to me talking about don't leave, he just showed up unannounced and it's me who she really wants to be with. I was like hell no I'm out of here and walked to the elevator.

Next thing I know he is coming down the hall. I jumped on the elevator and left. I called her last night when I got home, and she came over. She had listed me as a witness to the shooting incident that occurred in your building. I wanted her to know I was summoned to court about this incident and because the elevator door was shut, I couldn't testify that I witnessed the man shooting in our direction. She asked to stay over because she is afraid to go home, and so I let her, but nothing happened. I was moving her car over when you pulled up. Mari is fucked up and fucked up shit seems to follow her wherever she goes. I'm done with her ass and I am serious!"

I'm on my way to Noble's and I can't wait to tell him about all this mess. The only good part about this story is Dominica. She is truly the person that we all know and love. I knew it was too good to be true, she can't remember anything. I should go by to see Twaab. I'm going to call first.

"Hey sister, how are you doing?"

"I'm good just lying down thinking about how stupid I was, I heard you went to see Natasha Janine. How is she?"

"She's good! You can call her yourself and check on her. You all are friends and that's what friends do."

"Virg, you don't have to pay for the damages. I will get her car repaired with the money I have saved."

"Okay, I was going to stop up there. Do you need anything?"

"No sister, I'm good. Zam is up here now, and MJ is on her way. You can go home. Can you come up here tomorrow and bring Dominica up here with you? She's talking about she doesn't have any money and MJ won't return her calls."

"Why isn't MJ returning her calls?" MJ knows dang well she could call her back. She makes me sick when she does this to her.

"I don't know, and you know how they are?" I definitely do and they are a whole mess.

"Okay I will call Dominica and see if she is ok."

"Okay sister, I'll call you later."

I call Dominica and she answers before it rings. I say immediately to her, "Hey sister!"

"Virgie, what's that noise in the background?"

"Dominica, it's the wind because I'm on a speaker phone in my car."

"Aww, you scared me there. What's up Virgie?"

"Nothing I was checking on you."

"I'm good, I'm waiting on your sister to call me because I don't have any money."

"Who MJ?"

"Hell no, not MJ. Twaab said she was going to give me a couple of dollars."

"Dominica, how is Twaab going to give you some money from her hospital bed? Remember, she was in a car accident."

"My bad sister, I forgot, well I better call MJ's stingy ass. She never wants to give me any money. Who made her my payee anyway? Why couldn't you be my payee? Or Twaab? Whoever did this shit is fucked up? They are wrong for this." She is the one who told MJ that if she wasn't going to give her all of her money then keep the damn money. I'm sure she forgot that part of the story.

"Where are you, Dominica? I can bring you a couple of dollars?"

"I'm about to go up to Kelle's so you can meet me there. I am so hungry. I was going to go there to get something to eat since I can eat there for free. My whole family is fucking everyone who works there, and they feed me because of that." Well, I use to fuck the owner and our aunt is fucking the chef so I can't see the lie in that. I'm shaking my head laughing at her ass. "Yeah, Virgie meet me up there, okay sister! See you in a few.

117

I pull up to Kelle's and the place is packed as usual. I knew I would have to deal with his ass sooner or later and I definitely don't want Noble to have to do it. I park down the street and walk up to the hostess outside. I know her, I'm just bad with names.

"Hey girl, is my sister in there?" She is someone who use to hang out with Dominica.

"Yeah, Kelle just walked her in."

I walk in and see Dominica seated at a table in the front of the restaurant. She waves for me to come over there. I see Mr. Sid in the kitchen "working for wages" back there. I walk over to her table and here Kelle's clown ass comes over to us.

He says, "Hey Virg what brings you this way?"

Before I can answer my sister goes off. She has a short fuse, and it can be ignited in a blink of a second. Dominica says, "Man, cut that shit out. I just told your goofy ass she was meeting me up here. This is why she don't fuck with your ass no more; you just be saying shit to say some shit."

He looks at Dominica and says, "You sure did. Can I get you all something to eat?"

Dominica replies, "Yeah a short stock of banana pancakes, an order of bacon, a glass of orange juice and a glass of milk."

Now, this is my sister who makes me proud, she checked his ass.

Kelle asks, "Virgie what would you have?"

"Nothing thanks you."

"Virgie, are you okay? You seem as if something is wrong."

"Kelle, everything is not okay. Can I speak with you?"

"Sure, let's go to my office." I tell Dominica that I will be right back.

"Virg, you want me to kick his ass? You know I will."

"No, I got it but thanks."

Kelle is looking at us like what happened.

We are standing in his office and I sit at his desk.

"What's wrong my Virgie?"

"First of all, let's get some shit straight off the top. I am not your damn Virgie! You fucked that up when you thought spending every waking moment in this restaurant was the intimacy our relationship needed. Secondly, stay the fuck out of my business. What I do, who I am doing it with, where I choose to go, and whom I am going with is none of your damn business. Thirdly, if you feel the need to care about me and how hard I love, do me a solid and don't. You will fuck around and get your ass beat for nothing. I have been nothing but respectful of your ex-wife, your daughter, your restaurant, and your business. What have you done? You've tried to fuck up all of my business. Leave me the fuck alone and my family. Don't use my people to get closer to me. I was your friend until you tried this bullshit, but that's over now. I mean it, stay the fuck away from me and I will do the same."

I stood up to walk from behind his desk and was making my way to the door when he said, "Virgie I'm sick and miserable. I miss you and I just realized I fucked us up and I wish I could change things. I haven't told Cheryl and Nuri. You are the only person I have told."

"Kelle's what do you mean you are sick?"

"I'm having problems with my heart and they are running tests."

"Kelle I'm sorry to hear this, but it doesn't change how I feel. You need to tell your ex-wife and child. I need to move on with my life if I can even have a shot at happiness. I found someone who makes me immensely happy, and you put that in jeopardy with your lies and mind manipulation shit."

"How did I do that?"

"Kelle, by lying!"

"Virgie, I lied about what?"

"You never brought food over to his apartment?"

"No, I didn't!"

"So Kelle, you lied!"

"Okay what else did I lie about?"

"What do you mean by "what else?" Kelle, that's enough for me."

"I was jealous to see how happy you are, how amazing you have been looking, and how you are moving forward with your life. Virgie you can understand why I would want to mess that thing up. I love you and feel like no one deserves you more than me."

"Kelle when I needed to hear you say that you never did. I'm sorry for what's happening in your life. But you need to stay the fuck out of my business."

I walk out of the door before he tells me some more sad shit.

Dominica is sitting at the table with Mr. Sid.

"Hey Mr. Sid!"

"Hello Ms. Virgie, I want to apologize for my behavior."

"Mr. Sid, no need for an apology. Auntie explained it all and all is forgiven."

"Okay thank you. The meal for you all is on the house."

I say, "Oh you don't have to do that."

Dominica says, "The hell he doesn't. He is making this food so why can't we eat it for free."

I roll my eyes at her and say, "Thank you again, Mr. Sid."

As he is walking away Dominica says, "Yawl be too easy on the working men. They got jobs so paying for a meal or two is the least they can do. I say fuck them and keep going."

"Girl, shut the hell up, when all your damn men are unemployed with link cards."

"Damn Virg, I did say too hard on the working men not the unemployed men they don't have anything to give. You are coldblooded for talking about them, man they out here struggling." I had to laugh at that.

I'm on my way to Noble's this time for real. I dropped Dominica off at her place. I have to tell Noble about this day. He is not going to believe it. I use my keys to get into the building and the apartment. Noble is sitting at the table eating.

"Baby I can't wait to tell you about everything that happened today."

"Virgie, I haven't seen you all day and the first thing you want to do is talk."

"Yes Noble, a lot has happened today."

"Well babe all I want to do is..."

I interrupt him and finishes his sentence saying, "I know something sensual and nasty to me." He chuckles and says, "All I want to do is hug you because I missed you."

"Aww, I'm sorry Mr. Noble," and I give him a big hug.

He then kisses me on my forehead and says, "I do want to do something sensual to you, but I can wait until you finish telling me about your day."

I give him the pouty lips and smile to say to myself this man, this man.

"What am I going to do with you Mr. Noble?"

"I will tell you later but for now you have the floor."

I tell him everything from what Auntie had said about me being judgmental and how she wants to meet him. I tell him about Natasha Janine's drama, Twaab, Dominica and what happened at Kelle's.

The first thing he says is, "So Dominica really doesn't get the story right. I'm glad I found that out early. I see I am going to have to check Kelle's ass myself because he is still playing games."

"Noble, what about Natasha Janine and Raq?"

"Babe I knew about that already."

"What?" You knew and didn't tell me a thing. Wow, I'm always the last to know everything."

"Raq told me about it because he was surprised Natasha Janine knew those chicks. Raq said that's what they do."

"What do you mean that's "what they do?"

"They are high price escorts to men. They work together." I knew they were some hoes when Natasha Janine was telling me story.

"But you know the girl Mari is Mr. Corine's daughter?"

"I knew that too." Damn, he is a wealth of hidden knowledge. He sure can keep a secret.

"How did you know?"

"Raq hooked her up with Jon." This bitch is making her rounds.

"Who is Jon?" He is acting like I know these damn people.

"Babe, Dr. Tapes!" Shut the damn door! He has something to do with this shit too. Noble ass better not tell me he knows her too.

"What?" I say to myself, "Damn, he is fine, and he is mixed up with their asses. Even though this has nothing to do with how he looks. I just needed to point that out about him being fine and all."

"Yeah, and she stole his Rolex watch and was trying to sell it back to him." See, when you are lying you will definitely steal. I hope she didn't steal nothing from Natasha Janine.

"Are you serious?"

"Yes!" And, she isn't a petty thief, this bitch is stealing expensive shit.

Wow!

"But still how did you know she was Mr. Corine's daughter?"

"Because remember the night he needed my help. We went to your building to pick the watch up from her."

"What?" You all went to my building; I wish I had some tea right now.

I need something to drink listening to this shit.

"Yes, and she sent your neighbor who is her dad with the watch to give to Jon."

"Noble, did he pay her for the watch?" Mr. Corine, nosey ass didn't tell that.

"Hell no!"

"Noble, so how did he get it back?"

"Babe, Jon told her he would leak her medical records if she didn't give the watch back."

"Noble, he can't do that. It is unethical."

"Babe, he wasn't going to do it, but she became spooked about him saying that and gave him his watch back. Now, Jon is all stressed out because he thinks she may be passing something around to the men and women she is dating."

"Wow! This is terrible!"

"Yes, it is babe."

Now we are sitting here laughing at everything we just discussed and Noble says, "So where do you want to receive this while pointing to himself?"

"Mr. Noble, right on this table."

"Really babe? Let's clean it off."

"Mr. Noble, nope knock all of this stuff on to the floor." And before I could finish, he wiped the table clean.

"Virgie, tonight I need you to be the narrator okay."

"Okay!" I stand up from the chair and walk towards where he was sitting and say, "This cushion needs to feel your tongue as the fucking instrument," as I start crawling on top of the table. I know he doesn't like the word "fucking," but I'm in charge of this soliloquy so I will say what I want. He stands up and starts to pull at my pants while I am crawling on it.

"Mr. Noble, you need to roll your tongue up and push it into my cushion opening."

And he does just what I have demanded.

I say all seductively, "Now suck and lick this cushion clean. I will need you to move when I move to the edge of this table. Help me by crawling up on this table with me. Remove your shorts and then remove this top as I point at my blouse."

"Mr. Noble unfastens this bra and squeezes these pillows firmly! Now use your mouth to suck and bite on my left button softly then move to my right leaving wet kisses all over them. Suck and suck on them until my milk fills up at my buttons making them hard for a flick of your tongue." And he does.

"Ouch Noble and do it harder," and he does. "Help me by sucking my neck softly and slow. Help me by thrusting your muscle with one stroke into me, making me grab the edge of the table to keep from falling. Thrust again and again! And again, and again then take it out. Help me by holding my legs up and pulling me to the edge of the table and thrusting your muscle into my cushion making me scream in delight," and he does.

"Help me by thrusting and thrusting and thrusting slowly then fast. Then slowly again meeting me at every stroke. Allow me to release all of this energy as I meet you at your release by helping you too!" And he does and does and does until there is nothing left to do.

Noble finally asks, "Who are you?"

I muster up the words after this exhilarating experience,

"I'm Virgie baby."

"Babe, my future wife!"

SATURDAY

I am awakened by the memory of what Noble said, "My future wife!" Now that is a term, I can get used to hearing. I like the sound of it too. I walk into a room and someone says, "Hello Mrs. Winston, I just have to tell you that your husband is quite the handsome fellow. Aren't you the lucky one?" No ma'am he is the lucky one. Let me stop playing and get up. I need to go see Twaab in the hospital and get some things ready for work next week. Seven whole days out of the office messing around in these chocolate soliloquies with this man. They were nothing short of adventures, a game changer, and head spinning. Today should be easy breezy. Everything I need to know was revealed and everyone is safe from harm.

"My future wife!" This man doesn't even know all he does for me. Hello, I am Mrs. Virgie Mae Winston, I'm here to see my husband, Dr. Winston. Yes! Listen to how that sounds. Oo wee, I'm super excited and it hasn't happened yet. I believe you have to see yourself in the future. Look at Noble, sleeping like a baby because his future wife worked his ass out. He thinks he is wearing me out, but baby, I'm really wearing him out. I should wake him so we can act out another soliloquy. I used to think it was weird to be doing this. We are changing up the names for our body parts and acting out scenes from our imagination. We give each other intense passion. Often times, we are taking the role of a narrator. Providing specific instructions on what we need for the most pleasurable moments we can have with each other. I love our "chocolate soliloquies" now! Noble loves theater so the first time we were intimate he asked me to have an open mind about our sexual journey.

I remember sitting on his couch and with all these glass windows I mean, glass walls. It was a little chilly. He asked me if I wanted a blanket, and he turned the fireplace up. I felt like he had staged all this for me because we had been dating for a couple of weeks, and he was always very respectful. There were many nights, I went home hot and bothered because we didn't have sex. I would even say, deprived sex. I was not going to rush into anything. I had my fair share of disappointing encounters. I was determined to take it slow. I had just ended my relationship with Kelle, and not dating anyone. I was not rushing back into a serious relationship. I was really head over heels for Kelle, but our relationship became lacking. It was lacking in the areas of intimacy, romance, spontaneity, adventure, and travel outside of his restaurant. Then this man, this man came into my life right when I needed him. Noble would often point out how he desperately needed that hug I gave him the first time we met. But the truth of the matter is he doesn't know how much I needed it. That hug truly changed my life.

We were sitting under that blanket, under the heat from the fireplace, and from the chill of the room. We were talking, laughing, and having a great time. I kept saying to myself, "I'm getting me some today. He is not taking me home all hot and bothered today."

Noble asked me that day, "Is it okay for you to lay in my arms?" And then explained, "I want to feel you against my chest."

He was so sweet and soft. I used to think that he was gay and trying to connect with women. How crazy does that sound, but it's true. I really thought that about him. So, I moved closer to him and laid in his arms. We continued talking and laughing. We were really enjoying each other's company. He had prepared a beautiful meal for us and we both were stuffed. We ate roasted chicken breast, pasta in a garlic sauce, garlic bread, and broccoli. I will never forget it because everything we ate had garlic on it. I said to him, "I am too embarrassed to be speaking." He asked why and I told him because I was trying to make a good impression on him, and my breath smelled so bad.

He said, "I don't care how your breath smells. My impression of you won't change."

So, I was lying in his arms against his chest and while I was talking, he leaned in and kissed me. It was as if he was trying to suck the words out of my body. We had kissed before and passionately, but that kiss was quite different. It reminded me of our first hug. I didn't want him to let me go. I was so horny I immediately started touching his body. I was rubbing his back so fast because I thought he would stop me and take me home, so I wanted to get my feels first. He stopped kissing me and said, "Baby, slow down. We have time. There is no need to rush to do this."

I said, "Okay," because I thought that meant we will fuck next time. I was disappointed again, so I just kept kissing him. He laid my head on the couch and then came from under the blanket and got on top of me. I said to myself, "You are not wrong, he is about to give it to you."

While he was on top of me, he asked "How do you feel about sex?"

I answered, "I love it!"

Noble then said, "If you love it, are you willing to do it differently with me?"

I didn't know what he meant, but I was so horny I said, "Yes I am!"

He said, "I want you to view your body as a soft delicate possession."

He pointed to my breast and said, "These here are pillows I would love to bury my head in while I squeeze and play with them any way I want." He then said, "This right here, which was his first time touching my vagina, is a sweet muscle that controls it all. And this thing underneath is the cushion you use to sit on," squeezing my derrière.

I said, "What are we calling your penis?"

"Exactly what it is. My long, strong, and hard muscle," he said.

I'm so stupid I said, "Okay," smiling like a new student who was learning her anatomy for the first time.

He stood up and then pulled me up so I could be face to face with him. I became bashful about the breath thing and this weird play on words we were doing.

We were standing in the middle of the floor and he said, "It is your power I seek! Virgie, you are strong, independent, accomplished, successful, beautiful, smart, witty and sexy as hell. So, I need your power to fuel me. You have walked in this room and all I can imagine is experiencing your power as I connect with your body. I see the rise of your buttons as your pillows fill up with milk ready to be suckled for lactation. I am ready to exert my power over you. I am ready to thrust all of my power within your sweet muscle. Slowly then quickly making you scream without air. Will my power be too much for you to bear? This is the question I will ask myself. But I know after that first thrust you will gather your strength and meet me where we are. If I tell you we need to slow down or stop, will your power decrease? If I continue to do it slowly, will that allow you to savor in our moment? My goal is to have this moment too hard for you to forget my power. The power of my muscle is so strongly intense that it will ignite your sweet muscle making it drip so uncontrollably. The last words I want to hear from you, will be, "Noble, don't stop giving me your power!"

And when he did, I would say it over and over again. And over again. This man, this man!

It wasn't long before these moments would be named chocolate soliloquies. When I asked him why he named our moments together, he said it was because he wanted us to own our time. Noble said that our moments together are smooth like silk and dark like chocolate, and it is what we share with each other.

I said to him, "I thought it reminded you of me," jokingly. He said, "Babe, I don't need anything to remind me of you, you're always on my mind."

I would tell myself, "Virgie, this black man is so unbelievable. The things he says and do, you have never heard of a man doing in your life. He is so sensual, sexy and exotic."

I would call Natasha Janine and say, "Girl he is all of that and every day I pinch myself to see if I'm dreaming."

I felt as if I have waited all my life for him. I had all of those bad relationships, heartaches, disappointments, and unfortunate encounters that led me to this man. He is loving, thoughtful, sexy as hell, tall, dark, gorgeous, educated, attentive, and has all of his teeth. He doesn't have any children, no ex-wife drama, no crazy mother, nothing that would make me run for the door. I need to thank the love gods because they definitely "blessed" me. I am still in awe with this play on words.

Noble wakes up and says, "Morning babe, how long have you been awake?"

I say, because I can't really recall, "Just a little while."

"Babe, you are just laying here thinking. What's wrong?"

"Nothing I'm just laying here reminiscing on when all of this began."

"Babe, you must be reminiscing about the night when I threw that power on you. I had you begging me for more. I wore your sweet muscle out that night. I have been trying to top that night, ever since."

"Noble, you know what, just be quiet and go back to sleep."

"Babe okay, you know I did!"

"What are we doing today?"

"I want to go see Twaab at the hospital."

"Okay let's get up and eat so I can take my medicine and I will drive us there."

"Okay! Thank you, Mr. Noble."

"Do you want me to take a shower with you Virgie? I know how that power needs to be rejuvenated."

"Mr. Noble, I am fine, thank you for the suggestion. I can take a shower by myself without any assistance or spectators."

"Oh okay! Then I will be in bed saving my power for later, let me know when it's my turn."

"I sure, will!" This man, this man.

We are up, ready, and eating breakfast in a matter of an hour. Noble was driving so I was able to relax. I wore jogging pants, but they were the loose-fitting kind.

He says, "Babe you only wore those jogging pants because you don't want me to be distracted. It's too late I know what's really inside of those pants so I will stay distracted."

"Mr. Noble, focus on the road because this lady needs to get there unharmed."

"Okay unharmed, you need to hope we make it out of the hospital parking lot."

"Now Mr. Noble, this lady will be dropped off at the door. You won't dare ask me to walk from the parking lot, would you?"

"Ms. Lady, you are right. We will save the parking lot for a later date."

Noble has dropped me off at the main entrance of the hospital and I am walking inside. I stop at the receptionists' desk and say, "I am here to visit Twaab Kelly in room 1500." The receptionist tells me she already has two guests visiting at this time, and I will have to wait until someone comes down before I could go to her room. I stand in the reception area and wait for Noble. I call her room to see who is up there.

"Twaab, who is up there with you? Oh, okay tell them me and Noble are downstairs so they can send the passes down here and we all can visit together. Okay, we are down here waiting. I will see you soon."

Noble walks up and asks why I am not upstairs. I tell him that they have four people already up there and Zam is about to bring the passes down so we can go up.

"Babe, I thought it was only two visitors per patient."

"It is but stick with us, we know what we are doing."

Zam walks up and hands me the visitor passes. I tell Noble to start walking and that I am right behind him. I catch up to Noble, and we are now on our way up to Twaab's room. Noble will be totally surprised.

When we walk into the room, we are greeted by Dominica and MJ. My Auntie Kat (short for Katerina) was sitting in the chair next to the window.

I turn to Noble and say, "Now, you will meet my whole family."

While giving my Auntie a hug I then say, "Hey Auntie this is Noble."

He says, "Hello it's a pleasure to meet you."

"Hell, the pleasure is all mine with your fine ass. Turn around, let me get a good look at you," says Auntie.

Noble turns around and gives me this goofy look on his face. I'm cracking up.

She says, "I hear you are Mr. Doctor Love and the reason why we can't see my niece anymore."

"Ma'am, well I will take that credit."

"It doesn't look like you are taking anything, only giving it out," she says as she is flirting with my man.

"Auntie stop you are embarrassing this man," says MJ.

"MJ shut your ass up, you are the only person embarrassed here. This man is a love machine and Virgie already told me." I have never told her any of the sort even though it's true.

She continues by saying, "The only person in here isn't fucking is, you" and Twaab immediately interjects and says, "And me!" Auntie then says, "Twaab then that's your damn fault since you haven't given your damn life to Christ. We shouldn't be feeling sorry for your ass not getting none, you picked that road that is less traveled. MJ is the one who vowed to never touch a man."

"I haven't vowed anything. I'm waiting to marry the right person and do it the right way."

"MJ, you can wait until you are blue in the face and still end up with the wrong man, shit. I know because I have been there two times already and neither one of their asses was deserving of me."

I was so glad when I saw Dr. Tapes walk in the room. He taps Noble on his shoulder. Noble turns around and gives him the handshake and that brotherly embrace.

Dr. Tapes says, "Hello Ms. Virgie, Ms. Twaab. I haven't had the chance to formally introduce myself. I'm Jon, one of Noble's good friends. You are?" He says to MJ.

She says, "I'm Marion."

"Marion, bitch I never heard you use your birth name. This mother fucker got you sinning." My Auntie says while shaking her head at MJ.

Dominica gets up from the chair and says, "I'm Dominica and these are my sisters and that's my crazy Auntie Kat..."

"That's Ms. Katerina to you, young strong black man," she says interjecting Dominica.

"Now, this is something to take note of since he is probably the first person to never have had to ask you to talk with common sense," says MJ while rolling her eyes at Auntie.

Everybody starts laughing.

"Dr. Tapes I thought you work in the emergency room," I say.

He replies, "I do, but Dr. Winston told me he would be stopping by, so I came to see my brother."

"Oh okay!"

"Well, you all enjoy your visit and Ms. Twaab I hope you are healing nicely."

"Thank you."

Noble asks us to excuse him and go into the hall with Jon.

"Virgie Mae, how the hell do you meet all these fine ass men who are friends and doctors? And, your sister, MJ's ass almost fell on her damn face talking about my name is Marion. Yawl bitches are going to give me a heart attack."

"Auntie, please stop all that cursing?" MJ asks.

"MJ shut the hell up!"

I say, "Twaab what are they saying about your recovery?"

"Virgie, they want me to go to physical therapy when I'm discharged from here."

"Twaab, how is your mind?"

"Virgie, why are you asking about her mind and not about her leg and toes? They are the ones broke," says Dominica.

"Dominica, you're a damn fool! She is asking because those types of injuries can take a toll on a person's mind. I hope when you were in school, that they weren't just passing your ass on your looks alone. Because if that is the case, you need to go back and get some grades," says Auntie.

I'm dying laughing. This old lady is a fool.

"Auntie it's time to take you back home, this is too much stimuli for you," says MJ.

"So, what you're saying MJ is I'm getting on your last damn nerve. I hope it's true because you were down there at that church, so long. I forgot you even had nerves, or feelings, or even a pulse for whatever it's worth."

"Yep, it's time for her to go, I can't take it any longer." MJ says as she is grabbing Auntie's purse and bag.

Noble returns to the room and Auntie say, "Noble help your auntie up out of this chair."

Noble walks over to the chair to help her up by extending his arms to assist her and Auntie says, "Thank you so much!" She then winks at me as a sign of approval.

Auntie then says, "I bet you could have lifted me straight out of that chair with these big strong arms."

Dominica and I both bust out laughing. MJ is standing there rolling her eyes and Twaab is just smiling.

"Only if Ms. Virgie gave me permission to do so."

"Well, I wouldn't dare ask her that." Auntie says this while winking at me and sticking her tongue out of her mouth. He knows she is just flirting with him.

"Twaab, Noble and I are going to get out of here too. I will send Zam back. We are going to walk out with MJ and Auntie."

"Thank yawl for coming up here, I really appreciate it. I was thoroughly entertained."

"Okay sister, I will call you later."

We all are walking out. We step on the elevator. Auntie is still saying crazy things, but MJ keeps drowning her out so we really can't understand. MJ says to Noble, "Your friend seems so young? How old is he?"

"Jon is 48," answers Noble.

"Really?" MJ says.

"Just ask if the damn man is single?" Auntie interjects while rolling her eyes at MJ then smiles at me.

Noble says before she could ask, "He is single and a man of faith."

"Now you know, so what the hell are you going to do?" Auntie asks MJ.

I'm just laughing. This old lady is too funny. The elevator door opens and Noble tells me he is going to get the truck. MJ parked up front so they could walk straight to the car. Noble helps Auntie inside. Auntie is waving and smiling at me then gives me the thumbs up as an approval for Noble. Noble then closes the door and proceeds to get his truck.

Noble has already pulled up to the main entrance door in his Ford F-150 by the time MJ is pulling off. I can't understand why someone so sexy would drive a pickup truck. He should be in some flashy sports car with a custom paint job. He told me when I asked him a while back why did he drive a pickup truck he said, "I hate speed, but I love durability."

Saturday

I'm walking out the door towards Noble when I spot an attorney I worked with before. We worked on a civil case a couple of years back. She is walking out the main entrance door right behind me. She sees me and walks straight towards me. I stop and notice that she has a strange expression on her face. As I stop to recall her name, I'm reminded that it escapes me, so you know I did the "Hey, lady!" How have you been?"

She didn't respond because she was now staring at Noble as he was walking up. I'm saying to myself, "Yes that's my man and every piece of him."

Noble has walked towards us and says, "Hey Sarah! Do you know my Virgie?"

He then leans in and gives me a wet kiss. Oh yeah, now I remember. Sarah! That's her name. She is Sarah McDonald, attorney at law. How did I forget her name? We would joke on the breaks during the trial about how her name reminded us of Ronald McDonald. But how does Noble know her is what I'm thinking.

Sarah interrupts my thought and says with this astonished look on her face, "Noble I thought you were dead! Where have you been? How are you? What happened? Are you well? We were looking for you and no one knew anything. We tried to make contact at your last known address. I have so many questions. I'm so happy to see you."

Sarah extends her arms out to hug Noble, but he instead walks away. He walks behind me and hugs me by the waist kissing my neck. He says to Sarah, "I know I had you all worried, but I am doing great and moving on with my life. Please tell everyone I send my love and if you would excuse us, I want to take this lovely lady home so we can get some rest. It's been a long day. Sarah, it was good to see you too and maybe one day soon we can have lunch."

Sarah says, "I would like that, and you all have a good night." I say to myself, "What the hell is going on here. What the fuck just happened? What the fuck? Oh my God!"

Noble opens the truck door and helps me in. I see Sarah still standing on the sidewalk. I know she is thinking, "What the fuck is going on?" Why would she think he was dead? How does she know him? Did they use to date? Maybe even worse, were they secret lovers? I'm engrossed with questions in my head. When Noble reaches over to touch my hand and I nearly jump through the window.

He immediately pulls over and says, "Babe, are you okay? I know you have questions. I will answer them all but tell me you are okay because you are scaring me."

"Noble, I'm not okay because that conversation scares the hell out of me."

"Babe I know, and I never intended for you to ever be caught off guard by this information."

"Noble, what fucking information? What the fuck just happened? Who the fuck is "we"? Why would people think you are dead? What the fuck, is going on here? Who, the fuck, are you? Who the fuck is Dr. Noble Winston?